***"This is my proof,"* Karen murmured, still dazed.**

"Proof of what?"

"That you're a scoundrel and a thief. You stole that kiss," she accused, managing to get the words out with a straight face.

Laughter filled the air.

"Maybe the first one, darlin'," Grady conceded. "But the second one you gave me of your own free will. You can't count that one against me. Once two people start to tango, so to speak, the blame pretty much falls by the wayside."

She frowned at him. "You would say that, wouldn't you? It serves your purpose."

"And what is my purpose?" he asked, studying her with mild curiosity.

"To get my land," she said at once, but she was no longer as certain as she had once been. A part of her was beginning to believe that he just might be after *her,* instead....

Dear Reader,

Silhouette Books publishes many stars in romance fiction, but now we want to make *you* a star! Tell us in 500 words or less how Silhouette makes love come alive for you. Look inside for details of our "Silhouette Makes You A Star" contest—you could win a luxurious weekend in New York!

Reader favorite Gina Wilkins's love comes alive year after year with over sixty Harlequin and Silhouette romances to her credit. Though her first two manuscripts were rejected, she pursued her goal of becoming a writer. And she has this advice to offer to aspiring authors: "First, read everything you can, not just from the romance genre. Study pacing and characterization," Gina says. "Then, forget everything you've read and create something that is your own. Never imitate." Gina's *Bachelor Cop Finally Caught?* is available this month. When a small-town reporter is guilty of loving the police chief from afar and then tries to make a quick getaway, will the busy chief be too busy with the law to notice love?

And don't miss these great romances from Special Edition. In Sherryl Woods's *Courting the Enemy,* a widow who refused to sell her ranch to a longtime archrival has a different plan when it comes to her heart. *Tall, Dark and Difficult* is the only way to describe the handsome former test pilot hero of Patricia Coughlin's latest novel. When Marsh Bravo is reunited with his love and discovers the child he never knew, *The Marriage Agreement* by Christine Rimmer is the only solution! *Her Hand-Picked Family* by Jennifer Mikels is what the heroine discovers when her search for her long-lost sister leads to a few lessons in love. And sparks fly when her mysterious new lover turns out to be her new boss in Jean Brashear's *Millionaire in Disguise!*

Enjoy this month's lineup. And don't forget to look inside for exciting details of the "Silhouette Makes You A Star" contest.

Best,

Karen Taylor Richman,
Senior Editor

Please address questions and book requests to:
Silhouette Reader Service
U.S.: 3010 Walden Ave., P.O. Box 1325, Buffalo, NY 14269
Canadian: P.O. Box 609, Fort Erie, Ont. L2A 5X3

Sherryl Woods

Courting the Enemy

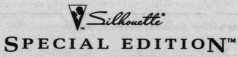

SPECIAL EDITION™

Published by Silhouette Books

America's Publisher of Contemporary Romance

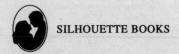 SILHOUETTE BOOKS

ISBN 0-373-24411-8

COURTING THE ENEMY

Visit Silhouette at www.eHarlequin.com

Printed in U.S.A.

Books by Sherryl Woods

SHERRYL WOODS

has written more than seventy-five romances and mysteries in the past twenty years. And because she loves to talk to real people once in a while, she also operates her own bookstore, Potomac Sunrise, in Colonial Beach, VA, where readers from around the country stop by to discuss her favorite topic—books. If you can't visit Sherryl at her store, then be sure to drop her a note at P.O. Box 490326, Key Biscayne, FL 33149.

Winding River High School
Class of '91

Welcome Home——Ten Years Later
Do You Remember the Way We Were?

Karen (Phipps) Hanson — Better known as The Dreamer. Elected most likely to see the world. Member of the 4-H club, the Spanish and French clubs, and first-place winner at the county fair in the greased pig contest.

Cassie Collins — Ringleader of the Calamity Janes. Elected most likely to land in jail. Best known for painting the town water tower a shocking pink and for making the entire faculty regret choosing teaching as a profession. Class record for detentions.

Gina Petrillo — Tastiest girl in the class. Elected most popular because nobody in town bakes a better double chocolate brownie. Member of the Future Homemakers of America. Winner of three blue ribbons in the pie-baking contest and four in the cake-baking contest at the county fair.

Emma Rogers — That girl can swing…a bat, that is. Elected most likely to be the first female on the New York Yankees team. Member of the Debate Club, the Honor Society and president of the senior class.

Lauren Winters — The girl with all the answers, otherwise known as the one you'd most like to be seated next to during an exam. Elected most likely to succeed. Class valedictorian. Member of the Honor Society, County Fair Junior Rodeo Queen and star of the junior and senior class plays.

Prologue

Soul-deep weary, Karen walked into the kitchen at midnight, made herself a cup of tea and sat down at the kitchen table to face the mail. She mentally weighed the usual stack of bills against the intriguing envelope with its fancy calligraphy.

Even if she hadn't desperately needed a pick-me-up, she would have opted for setting the bills aside. There were always too many of them at the end of the month and not enough money in the bank. It seemed as if she and Caleb might never get their ranch in the black, might never be in a position to hire the extra help that would save them from doing all of the endless, backbreaking work themselves with only two seasonal men to pitch in.

As late as it was, she had just come in from the barn. Caleb was still out there, trying to save a sick calf. Always at the edge of bankruptcy, they couldn't afford to lose a single animal. She had seen the stress in his face, heard it in the terse, angry words from a man who'd always been quietly thoughtful and even-tempered.

She pushed all of that aside as she opened the thick vellum envelope, and removed what turned out to be an invitation to her high school reunion in Winding River, Wyoming, a hundred miles away. Immediately the cares of the day slipped aside. She thought of her lifelong friends, the women who had called themselves the Calamity Janes, thanks to their penchant for heartbreak and mischief gone awry.

This was perfect. A few days with her best friends would give her marriage exactly the boost it needed. It would bring some fun back into their lives. Though Caleb was older and hadn't gone to school with them, he had grown to enjoy their company as much as she did. And because he was the only husband who'd displayed staying power, they fussed over him in a way that both embarrassed and pleased him.

She was still thinking about catching up with Cassie, Gina, Lauren and Emma, when Caleb finally came in. She studied his face and tried to gauge his mood. Wordlessly he opened the refrigerator and took out a beer, slugging it back as if his throat were parched. Finally he glanced at her, then at the envelope she was holding.

"What's that?"

"An invitation. My high school class is having its reunion in July." She beamed at him. "Oh, Caleb, it's going to be such fun. I'm sure Gina, Lauren and the others will come back. There are going to be all sorts of events, a picnic, a dance, plus the town's annual fireworks on the Fourth."

"And how much is all of this going to cost? An arm and a leg, I imagine."

His tone dulled her enthusiasm. "Not so much. We can manage it."

He gestured toward the stack of bills. "We can't pay the electric bill. The feed and grain bill is two months overdue—and you want to go to a bunch of fool parties? And where exactly would we stay now that your parents have moved? You planning on driving a hundred miles each way every single day? Motels are expensive."

"We need this," she insisted stubbornly. "I'll find us a place to stay."

"We need to hang on to every single dollar we can get our hands on, or this time next year we're going to be worrying about a place to live."

It was a familiar refrain, and it was Caleb's greatest fear. Karen knew that and she didn't take it lightly. It wasn't just a matter of holding on to the ranch he loved, the ranch that had been in his family for three generations. It wasn't even a matter of pride. It was a matter of keeping the ranch out of the hands of the man he considered his family's worst enemy.

Grady Blackhawk had been after the Hanson ranch for years, the entire time Karen had been with Caleb. She couldn't recall a week that there hadn't been some communication from him, some sense that he was circling like a vulture waiting for the ranch to collapse under Caleb's ineptitude. She didn't fully understand Grady's motivation, because Caleb had flatly refused to discuss it. He'd just painted him as the devil incarnate and warned Karen time and again against him.

"Caleb, we're not going to lose the ranch," she

said, clinging to her patience by a thread. "Not to Grady Blackhawk, not to anyone."

"I wish to hell I were as sure of that as you are. You want to go to your reunion, go, but leave me out of it. I have more important things to do with my time—like keeping a roof over our heads."

With that he had stormed out of the house, and she hadn't seen him again until morning.

She let the subject of the reunion drop, and a few days later, looking sheepish, Caleb apologized and handed her a check to pay for all of the events.

"You're right. We need this. We'll see all of your friends, maybe dance a little," he said, giving her a tired but suggestive wink that reminded her that they had fallen in love on a dance floor.

Karen pressed a kiss to his cheek. "Thank you. It's going to be wonderful. You'll see."

Instead, making up for time lost at the reunion turned out to be more than Caleb's heart could take. Only days after it was over, he collapsed.

She should have seen it coming, Karen berated herself en route to the hospital, should have known that no man could survive under so much self-imposed pressure.

Maybe if she hadn't been caught up with all of the Calamity Janes, she would have. Instead, though, she had stolen every spare minute to spend time with her best friends, time away from the ranch she could ill afford.

But with Emma working as a hotshot attorney in Denver at the time, Lauren lighting up the silver screen in Hollywood, with Gina running her exclusive Italian restaurant in Manhattan, and even Cassie living a few hundred miles away, Karen was determined to take advantage of every single second they were home. Seeing them rejuvenated her.

She was in Denver with Cassie, awaiting the results of her mother's breast cancer surgery, when the call came that Caleb was being taken to the hospital. A million and one thoughts raced through her mind on the flight to Laramie. Nothing her friends did or said could distract or reassure her. Guilt crowded in.

She had pressed Caleb to attend the reunion. She had left him alone to keep up with all of the ranch chores even after the events ended. It was little wonder that he had broken under the stress, and it was her fault. All of it. She would live with that forever.

But he would be all right, she told herself over and over. And she would make it up to him, work twice as hard from now on.

At the hospital, the doctor greeted her, his expression grim. "It was too late, Mrs. Hanson. There was nothing we could do."

Karen stared at him, not understanding, not wanting to believe what he seemed to be saying. "Too late?" she whispered as the Calamity Janes moved in close to offer support. "He's..." She couldn't even say the word.

Neither could the doctor, it seemed. He nodded, his tone conveying what his words merely hinted. "Yes. I'm sorry. The heart attack was massive."

Sorry, she thought wildly. There was plenty of regret to go around. She was sorry, too. She would spend a lifetime being sorry.

But being sorry wouldn't bring Caleb back. It wouldn't save the ranch from Grady Blackhawk. It was up to her to do that.

And she would, too, no matter what it took, no matter what sacrifices she had to make. After all, her husband had paid for that damnable ranch with his life.

Chapter One

The kitchen table was littered with travel brochures, all provided by Karen's well-meaning best friends. She sat at the table with her cup of tea and a home-made cranberry scone baked just that morning and dropped off by Gina, and studied the pictures without touching them. She was almost afraid to pick up the brochures, afraid to admit just how tempted she was to toss aside all of her responsibilities and run away.

The Calamity Janes had known just how to get to her, selecting all the places she had talked about back in high school. London, of course. Always her first choice since so much of her favorite literature had been written there. And Italy because of the art in Florence, because of the history in Rome and the ca-nals of Venice. Paris for the sidewalk bistros on shady streets and for the Louvre and Notre Dame. They had

thrown in a cruise through the Greek isles and a re-
laxing resort in Hawaii for good measure.

Once the images would have stirred her imagination, the prospect of actually being able to choose one
would have filled her with excitement, but today all
she felt was sadness. Finally, after all these years, she
could make her dream come true, but only because
her husband was dead, only if she turned her back on
everything that had mattered to him…to them.

Caleb was dead. The words still had the power to
shock her, even now, six months after his funeral.
How could a man not yet forty be dead? He had always appeared so healthy, so strong. Though he'd
been ten years older, she had been drawn to him from
the moment they met because of his vitality, his zest
for living. Who would have guessed that his heart was
weak…a heart that had been capable of such love,
such tenderness?

Tears welled up, spilled down her cheeks, splat-
tered on the glossy brochures for places she had put
off seeing to marry the man of her dreams.

Not a day went by that Karen didn't blame the
ranch for killing him. That and her stubborn determination to take time off for her high school reunion.
Six months hadn't changed her mind about where the
blame lay.

Nor had it dulled her grief. Her friends were worried about her, which explained the arrival this morning of all the brochures. They had remembered how
she had once talked of leaving Wyoming behind, of
becoming a flight attendant or a travel agent or a
cruise director, anything that would allow her to see
the world. They were using all of those old dreams
in an effort to tempt her into taking a break.

A break, she thought derisively. Her so-called break for that reunion was the reason Caleb was dead. Running a ranch didn't allow for breaks, not a ranch the size of hers anyway. It was a full-time, never-ending, backbreaking job, with often pitiful rewards.

Once she and Caleb had envisioned taking trips together, traveling to all the exciting, faraway places she had dreamed about before she'd met him and fallen in love. He had understood her dreams even if he hadn't shared them. This ranch had been his only obsession.

There had been other dreams, of course, ones they *had* shared. They had dreamed of filling the house with children, but they'd put it off. Just until finances took a turn for the better, he'd promised her.

Now there would be no children, she thought bitterly. No vacations to exotic locales. Not with Caleb, anyway. They'd never gone farther away from home than Cheyenne, where they'd spent their three-day honeymoon.

The Calamity Janes had obviously anticipated her protests that there was no money for a frivolous vacation, no time to indulge a fantasy. Her friends had prepaid a trip to anywhere in the world she wanted to go. It was Lauren's extravagant gift, most likely, Karen surmised. Lauren's and Emma's. Of Karen's high school classmates, the actress and lawyer were the only ones with any cash to spare right now.

Cassie had recently married a successful technology whiz, but their road was still rocky as Cole struggled to accept the fact that Cassie had kept his son a secret from him for years. Cassie wouldn't ask Cole for money, though Karen didn't doubt he would have offered if he'd known about the plan. Cole had been a rock since Caleb's death, pitching in to handle a hundred little details, things she would never have thought of. He'd wanted to do more, offered to send over extra help, but she had turned him down. Taking on the burden of running the ranch was her penance.

As for Gina, she had been in some sort of financial scrape with her New York restaurant that she flatly refused to discuss, but it was serious enough to have driven her out of New York and back to Winding River to stay. She spent her days in a frenzy of baking and her nights working in the local Italian restaurant where she'd first developed the desire to become a chef. There had been a handsome man hovering around ever since the reunion, but Gina steadfastly refused to introduce him or to explain his presence.

Karen loved them all for their support and their generosity. Her friends' hearts were in the right place, but she couldn't see how she could go to Cheyenne for a day trip right now, much less on some dream vacation. The work on the ranch hadn't died with her husband. Hank and Dooley were pitching in to take up the slack, but they were beginning to get nervous about how they'd be paid or whether the ranch would even survive. They were right to worry, too. Karen didn't have any answers for them. She knew, though, that Dooley, who'd worked with the Hansons for three decades, had persuaded the younger, more impulsive Hank to give her time to figure things out.

It was January now. She could tell them to find other work and manage for a while, but when spring came, she would have to have help once more. Better to scrape by and re-hire these two, whose loyalty she was sure of, than risk finding no one she could trust come April.

She groaned even as the thought crossed her mind. She was beginning to think like Caleb, seeing betrayal and enemies around every corner. He had been totally paranoid about Grady Blackhawk's designs on their ranch. It was true that Grady wanted it. He'd made no secret of the fact, especially since Caleb's death, but it was unlikely that he'd try to get it by planting a spy on her payroll.

Apparently she needed this break more than she wanted to admit. She finally dared to reach for the brochure on London and studied the photos of Buckingham Palace, the Old Vic, Harrods, the cathedrals.

She tried to imagine what London would be like in winter, with snow dusting the streets. Currier and Ives–style images from her favorite authors came to mind. It would be magical. It would be everything she'd ever dreamed of.

It was impossible.

She sighed heavily and reluctantly put the brochure down again, just as someone knocked at the kitchen door.

When she opened it, her heart thumped unsteadily at the sight of Grady Blackhawk. He'd been at the funeral, too. And he'd called a half-dozen times in the weeks and months since. She'd tried her best to ignore him, but he'd clearly lost patience. Now here he was on her doorstep.

"Mrs. Hanson," he said with a polite nod and a finger touched to the rim of his black Stetson.

She had the whimsical thought that he was deliberately dressing the part of the bad guy, all in black, but the idea fled at once. There was nothing the least bit whimsical about Grady. He was quiet and intense and mysterious.

The latter was a bit more of a problem than she'd anticipated when he first came to pay his respects after Caleb's death. Karen had always liked unraveling puzzles, and Grady was the most complicated one she'd ever run across. Unfortunately, sifting through clues, ferreting out motives took time, time she didn't dare spend with her husband's longtime enemy.

She could just imagine the disapproval of Caleb's parents, if they heard she was spending time with Grady Blackhawk. Word would reach them, too. She had no doubts about that. Most of the people in the area were far closer to the Hansons, who'd lived here for decades, than they were to Karen, who was still regarded as a newcomer even after ten years as Caleb's wife. The phone lines between here and Tucson would be burning up as the gossip spread.

"I thought I had made it clear that I have nothing to say to you," she told Grady stiffly, refusing to step aside to admit him. Better to allow the icy air into the house than this man who could disconcert her with a look.

This man, with his jet-black hair and fierce black eyes, was now her enemy, too. It was something she'd inherited, right along with a failing ranch.

She wished she understood why Grady was so desperate to get his hands on this particular ranch. He had land of his own in a neighboring county—plenty of it from what she'd heard. But there was something about Hanson land that obsessed him.

Over the years he—and his father before him—had done all he could to steal the Hanson land. Not that he wasn't willing to pay. He was. But, bottom line, he wanted something that wasn't rightfully his, and he intended to get it by fair means or foul.

According to Caleb, Grady had no scruples, just a single-minded determination. He'd tried to buy up their note at the bank, but fortunately, the bank president was an old family friend of Caleb's father. He had seen the paperwork, foiled the attempt, then dutifully rushed to report everything to the Hansons. That much was fact.

In addition—and far more damning—Caleb had been all but certain Grady was behind a virus that had infected half their herd the previous year. He had also blamed Grady for a fire that had swept through pastureland the year before that, destroying feed and putting the entire herd at risk.

There had been no proof, of course, just suspicions, which Karen had never entirely bought. After all, Grady had been waiting in the wings, checkbook in hand, after each incident. Would he have been foolish enough to do that if he'd been behind the acts in the first place? Wouldn't he know that he'd be the first person to fall under suspicion? Or hadn't he cared, as long as he got his way?

"I think it would be in both our interests to talk," he said, regarding her with the intense gaze that always disquieted her.

"I doubt that."

He ignored her words and her pointed refusal to back away from the door. "I've made no secret over the years of the fact that I want this land."

"That's true enough." She regarded him curiously. "Why *this* land? What is it about this particular ranch that made your father and now you hound the Hansons for years?"

"If you'll allow me to come inside, I'll explain.

Perhaps then you won't be so determined to fight me on this."

Karen's sense of fair play and curiosity warred with her ingrained animosity. Curiosity won. She stepped aside and let him enter. He removed his hat and hung it on a peg, then took a seat at the table. She took comfort in the fact that he didn't remove his coat. He clearly wouldn't be staying long.

His intense gaze swept the room, as if taking stock, then landed on the scattered brochures.

"Going somewhere?" he asked, studying her with surprise. "I didn't think you had the money to be taking off for Europe."

"I don't," she said tightly, wondering how he knew so much about her finances. Then again, just about everyone knew that she and Caleb had been struggling. "My friends do. They're encouraging me to take a vacation."

"Are you considering it?"

"Not with you circling around waiting for me to make a misstep that will cost me the ranch."

He winced at that. "I know how your husband felt about me, but I'm not your enemy, Mrs. Hanson. I'm trying to make a fair deal. You have something I want. I have the cash to make your life a whole lot easier. It's as simple as that."

"There is nothing simple about this, Mr. Blackhawk. My husband loved this ranch. I don't intend to lose it, especially not to the man he considered to be little better than a conniving thief."

"A harsh assessment of a man you don't know," he said mildly.

"It was his assessment, not mine. Caleb was not

prone to making quick judgments. If he distrusted you, he had his reasons.''

"Which you intend to accept blindly?''

It was her turn to wince. Loyalty was one thing, but her sense of fair play balked at blindly accepting anything.

"Persuade me otherwise,'' she challenged. "Convince me you had nothing to do with the attempts to destroy our herd, that your intentions were honorable when you tried to buy up the note on the land.''

He didn't seem surprised by the accusations. He merely asked, "And then you'll sell?''

"I didn't say that, but I will stop labeling you as a thief if you don't deserve it.''

He grinned at that, and it changed him from somber menace to charming rogue in a heartbeat. Karen nearly gasped at the transformation, but she wouldn't allow herself to fall prey to it. He hadn't proved anything yet. She doubted he could.

"If I tell you that none of that is true, not even the part about the mortgage, would you believe me?'' Grady asked.

"No.''

"What would it take?''

"Find the person responsible.''

He nodded. "Maybe I will. In the meantime, I'm going to tell you a story,'' he said in a low, easy, seductive tone.

His voice washed over Karen, lulling her as if it were the start of a bedtime story. She was tired enough to fall asleep listening to it, but she sat up rigidly, determined not to display any sign of weakness in front of this man.

"Generations ago this land belonged to my ancestors," Grady began. "It was stolen from them."

"Not by me," she said heatedly, responding not just to the accusation but to the fact that she'd dared to let down her guard for even a split second. "Nor my husband."

He seemed amused by her quick retort. "Did I say it had been? No, this was years and years ago, before your time or mine. It was taken by the government, turned over to homesteaders. White homesteaders," he said pointedly. "My ancestors were driven onto reservations, while people like the Hansons took over their land."

Karen was aware that much had been done to the Native Americans that was both heartless and wrong. She sympathized with Grady Blackhawk's desire to right an old wrong, but she and Caleb—or, for that matter, Caleb's parents and grandparents—weren't the ones to blame. They had bought the land from others, who, in turn, had simply taken advantage of a federal policy.

"You're asking me to make amends for something I had no part in," she told him.

"It's not a matter of paying an old debt that isn't yours. It's a matter of doing what's right because you're in a position to do so. And I certainly don't expect you just to give the land to me because I say it rightfully belongs to my family. I'll pay you a fair price for it, same as anyone else would. I guarantee it will be far more than what was paid for it all those years ago."

Before she could stop him, he named an amount that stunned her. It would be enough to pay off all their debts and leave plenty for her to start life over again back in Winding River, where she'd be with friends. It was tempting, more tempting than she'd imagined. Only an image of Caleb's dismay steadied her resolve. Keeping this ranch was the debt she owed to him. She could never turn her back on that.

"I'm not interested in selling," she said with finality.

"Not to me or not to anyone?" Grady asked with an edge to his voice.

"It hardly matters, does it? I won't sell this ranch."

"Because you love it so much?" he asked with a note of total disbelief in his voice.

"Because I can't," she responded quietly.

He seemed startled by the response. "It's not yours to sell?"

"Technically, yes. But I owe it to my husband to stay here, to do what he would have done, if he hadn't died so prematurely. This ranch will stay in Hanson hands as long as I have any control over it."

For a moment, he looked taken aback, but not for long. His gaze locked with hers, he said, "I'll keep coming back, Mrs. Hanson, again and again, until you change your mind or until circumstances force your hand. This place is wearing you down. I can see it." He gestured toward the brochures. "Obviously so can your friends. Make no mistake, I'll own the land…no doubt before the year is out."

His arrogant confidence stirred her temper. "Only if hell freezes over," she said, snatching the back door open and allowing a blast of wintry air into the room as she waited pointedly for him to take the hint and leave.

His gaze never wavered as he plucked his hat off the hook and moved past her. He paused just outside and a smile tugged at his lips. "Keep a close eye on the weather, Mrs. Hanson. Anything's possible."

Chapter Two

Grady hadn't expected Karen Hanson to be as stubborn or as foolish as her husband. After the funeral he'd made a few calls to test the waters, but he had deliberately waited six months before going to see her. He'd wanted to give her time to see just how difficult her life was going to be. He'd guessed that by now she would be eager to get rid of a ranch that was clearly draining whatever reserves of cash she had. Obviously he'd misjudged her. He wouldn't make that mistake again.

More disconcerting than the discovery that she wasn't going to be a pushover was the realization that she got to him. Those big blue eyes of hers had been swimming with tears when she'd opened the door. Her flushed cheeks had been streaked with them. Her lips had looked soft…and disturbingly kissable. He'd had an almost irresistible urge to gather her in his arms and offer comfort. For a hard man with little sympathy for anyone, it had been an uncharacteristic reaction that made him uneasy.

He grinned as he imagined her reaction to that. If he'd even tried to touch her, no matter how innocently, she probably would have grabbed an umbrella from the stand by the door and clobbered him with it.

Even so, he hadn't been able to shake that image of lost vulnerability. A lot of women who worked ranches side by side with their husbands grew hard, their muscles well formed, their skin burnished bronze by the sun. By contrast, Karen Hanson's body was soft and feminine, her skin as pale as milk. The thought of that changing because she had to struggle to keep her ranch afloat bothered him for reasons that went beyond her refusal to give in and sell out to him.

He couldn't help wondering what drove a woman like Karen Hanson. Well…loyalty to her husband, for one thing. There was no question about that. Pride. Stubbornness. He sighed. He was back to that again. It was hard to fight with someone who'd dug in her heels in defiance of logic.

But what did she long for beyond the travel that those brochures implied? In his experience most women wanted love, a family, the things he hadn't had time for in his own life. Some wanted a meal ticket. Some had a mile-wide independent streak, needing little more than the occasional companionship of a man to make them content. Those were the ones who appealed to Grady. He had so many family obligations to the past, he didn't have time to think about the future.

He tried to fit Karen Hanson into a tidy little niche,

but she wouldn't stay put. She was independent, no doubt about it, but her determination to fight her husband's old battles said a lot about how she felt about family. Ironically, that very loyalty, every bit as strong as his own commitment to his ancestors, was likely to stand in his way.

He had derided himself on the trip home for trying to analyze the woman based on a half-hour meeting that had been rife with tension. He knew better. His grandfather—the single greatest influence in his life—believed in the necessity for walking a mile in another man's moccasins before reaching conclusions about the choices they made. Thomas Blackhawk had tried to instill that same wisdom in Grady.

Unfortunately, Grady wasn't usually capable of the patience required. He tended to make snap judgments. He asked straight questions, liked straight answers.

"And look where that got you today," he muttered wryly. His grandfather would have been appalled, especially by the unveiled threat he had uttered on his way out the door.

He spent the evening taking stock, both of his own behavior and Karen Hanson's responses to it. Unfortunately, there was little definitive information to go on. She was beautiful, stubborn, hardworking and loyal. He'd gotten that, but not much more, certainly nothing about the best way to handle her.

There was only one way to remedy that. He needed to spend more time with her. He had to discover what made the woman tick, what her hopes and dreams were now that her husband was gone.

And how he could use it to his own advantage, he reminded himself sharply, when the image of her in his bed stole over him. He was going to have to keep that image at bay, he warned himself.

He'd spent his whole life working toward a single goal—getting that land back for his family. His great-grandfather had instilled a desire for retribution in his son, Grady's grandfather. The mission had been passed down to the next generation, and finally to Grady himself.

That land, part of his Native American heritage, part of a time when his ancestors had had no rights at all, was Blackhawk land. He couldn't let anything—not even a woman as desirable as Karen Hanson—distract him from getting it back while his grandfather was still alive to savor the triumph.

He chuckled dryly as he imagined how she was going to react to any attempt on his part to get to know her. She'd probably shoot him on sight if he showed up at the ranch again, especially if she guessed that his mission was to find her weaknesses and exploit them.

For once he was going to have to follow his grandfather's advice and rely on patience and maybe a little subterfuge to get what he wanted. There were a lot of chores around that ranch that needed doing. Karen struck him as a pragmatic woman. If he simply appeared one day and went to work, steering clear of her for the most part, would she run him off or accept the help because she knew she needed it? He was counting on the latter. Maybe over time, she would get used to his presence, come to accept it and allow him a little insight into her soul.

Grady lifted his beer in a silent toast to the ingenuity of his plan. By this time tomorrow he intended to have taken his first steps in Karen Hanson's shoes.

Of course, he admitted ruefully, it remained to be seen if he'd live to tell about it.

"Why not sell to him?" Gina asked as the Calamity Janes sat in the ranch kitchen eating pasta that she had prepared. The room was filled with the rich scent of garlic and tomato and basil. A plate of garlic bread had been all but demolished and there were only a few strands of spaghetti left in the huge bowl she had prepared for the five old friends.

Karen had put out an urgent call for their help within minutes of Grady Blackhawk's departure. She was counting on the Calamity Janes to give her advice and to keep her mind off the disconcerting effect his visit had had on her. Selling to Grady was not the advice she'd been expecting. She'd been hoping for some clever way to sidestep his determination permanently. That warning of his was still ringing in her ears.

"How can I sell to Grady?" Karen asked. "Caleb hated him. It would be the worst kind of a betrayal. And it would break his parents' hearts. Even though they've moved, they still think of this ranch as home."

"Do you want to spend the rest of your life struggling to keep the ranch afloat for two people who will never come back here? This place is a nostalgic memory for the Hansons. For you, it's nothing but backbreaking work," Cassie pointed out. "Don't forget, you were relieved when your own parents sold out and moved to Arizona. You said you'd never set foot on a ranch again." She grinned. "Of course, that was five minutes before you met Caleb, and from that moment on, all bets were off. You claimed to each and every one of us that you had always wanted to be a rancher's wife."

Karen frowned at the well-meant reminder. "No, to be perfectly honest, you're right. I don't want to be a rancher. I never did," she admitted. "But—"

Cassie cut her off. "Then consider Grady's offer if it's a fair one. Caleb would understand."

But Karen knew he wouldn't. The kind of enmity he had felt for Grady Blackhawk was deep and eternal. It was an emotional, gut-deep hatred that couldn't be abandoned in favor of practicality or sound business reasons or even sheer exhaustion, which was what she was beginning to feel as the endless days wore on.

"Okay, if the issue really comes down to keeping this place away from Grady Blackhawk, then *I'll* buy the ranch," Lauren said, drawing laughter.

"And what would you do with a ranch?" Karen asked, trying to imagine the big-screen superstar mucking out stalls or castrating bulls or any of the other backbreaking tasks required by ranching.

"You seem to forget that I grew up on a ranch, same as you," Lauren replied with a touch of indignation. "In fact, nobody around here had a better way with horses than I did."

"That was a long time ago. Somehow it's hard to picture now. It doesn't quite work with the glamorous image you've created in Hollywood," Cassie said.

Lauren scowled. "It could work if I wanted to make it work. This glamour stuff is highly overrated."

Karen thought she heard an increasingly familiar note of dissatisfaction in her friend's voice. She'd heard it when Lauren was home for the reunion, and it had continued to pop out from time to time on her return visits.

The fact that those return visits, even under the guise of checking up on Karen, were happening more and more frequently was telling. Lauren had done only one film in the past six months and turned down half a dozen offers. Compared to the pace of her career in the past, that was darned close to retirement.

"Okay, Lauren, spill it," Karen ordered. "What are you not telling us? Are you getting tired of being the multimillion-dollar superstar?"

"As a matter of fact, I am," Lauren said with a touch of defiance. "And you needn't look so shocked. I never intended to be an actress. I certainly never thought I'd be famous for my looks. I was the brainy one, remember? I wore glasses and had freckles and hair that wouldn't quite do what I wanted it to. I still do. Do you know that without my contacts and makeup and with my hair air-dried instead of styled, I can actually walk into a supermarket and no one looks twice at me?"

"Isn't that a good thing?" Karen asked. She had never been able to grasp how a woman as private and shy as Lauren had always been had learned to cope with fame.

"Yes, but it just proves how shallow the rest of my life is," Lauren said. "It's all built on lies. Don't get me wrong, I'm not whining."

"Yes, you are," they all said in a chorus, followed by laughter.

"Okay, maybe a little. I just want something more."

"A ranch?" Karen asked skeptically.

Lauren's expression set stubbornly. "Maybe."

Karen shook her head. "Let me know when you make up your mind for sure. Until then, I think I'll just hang on to this place."

"You know what I think?" Emma said, her too-perceptive gaze studying Karen intently. "I think Karen's just holding out so she can keep this Grady Blackhawk coming around." A grin spread across her face. "Have you seen this man? I remember him from the funeral. He is seriously gorgeous. All dark and brooding, with trouble brewing in his eyes."

"I hadn't noticed," Karen insisted, but she had. God help her, she had.

"Liar," Emma accused. "You'd have to be blind not to notice."

"It was my husband's funeral," Karen snapped. "I wasn't taking note of the sex appeal of his worst enemy."

"What about today?" Emma persisted. "Did you notice today?"

Since in typical attorney fashion, Emma wasn't going to let up until she got the confession she was after, Karen conceded, "Okay, he's a good-looking man. That doesn't make him any less of a scoundrel."

"Have you figured out just why Caleb hated the man so much?" Gina asked as she absentmindedly shredded the last piece of garlic bread into a little pile of crumbs.

"Because of the land, of course," Karen said. "Isn't that what we've been talking about?"

Gina was already shaking her head before Karen finished speaking. "I don't think so. There had to be more to it. I think this was personal."

"It's fairly personal when a man tries to buy up your mortgage so he has the leverage to take your land,'' Karen said. ''It's even more personal when you suspect him of trying to sabotage your herd of cattle.''

''I think there's more,'' Gina said stubbornly. ''Caleb was the nicest guy in the world. He loved everybody. He trusted everybody. He even liked Emma's ex-husband well enough, though heaven knows why. He got along with everybody—except Grady Blackhawk.''

''The bad blood between the Hansons and Blackhawks went back a lot of years,'' Karen reminded her. ''It was always over the land.''

''Maybe that's just what they said, maybe that was a cover for the real reason for the animosity,'' Gina said.

Karen sighed at her persistence. ''Okay, Gina, what do you think it was about?''

''I think there was a woman involved,'' Gina said at once. ''And a broken promise.''

The rest of them groaned.

''If you ever decide to give up the restaurant business, maybe you could write romance novels,'' Emma said. ''In this instance, it sounds to me as if you're reaching a bit.''

''More than a bit,'' Karen said. ''Can we change the subject?''

''You got us over here to talk about Grady,'' Emma reminded her. ''You said you wanted advice. I could always have a restraining order drawn up to keep him out of your hair.''

''Typical lawyer,'' Gina said with an undeniable trace of bitterness that ran awfully deep under the circumstances. ''Turn a simple situation into a legal brawl. All Karen has to do is tell the man she's not interested in his offer. Period.''

"Which I've done," Karen said.

"And you think that's the end of it?" Emma scoffed.

Karen thought of Grady's taunt as he'd walked out. No, unfortunately, she didn't believe it was over. He would be back. The only questions were when and what his tactics might be.

"He's not through," she admitted reluctantly. "He's not the kind of man who will give up easily. He's been after this land as long as I've known Caleb. And his father was after it before that. I doubt he took my refusal to sell all that seriously. In fact, it seemed to amuse him."

"All the more reason to sell to me," Lauren said. "I know how to deal with men like that. Hollywood is crawling with creeps who don't know how to take no for an answer."

"I'd love to hear how you handle them," Gina said, looking surprisingly despondent. "I've got one I'd like to shake."

Emma's gaze sharpened. "Care to explain that?"

"No," Gina said flatly. "But if Lauren has any techniques that are both legal and effective, I'd like to hear them."

"I can't talk with a lawyer present," Lauren joked. "She'd be duty-bound to turn me in."

"Illegal, then," Gina surmised. "I'll keep that in mind, if it comes to that."

Karen was about to jump all over the remark and demand answers, but a warning glance from Cassie silenced her. Maybe Cassie knew more of the story than the rest of them. She and Gina had always had a special bond, perhaps because they'd worked together so often when they were teens, both as waitresses, but with Gina always snooping around the kitchen, testing recipes of her own whenever she was given the chance.

"We're getting pretty far afield, anyway," Cassie said. "We need to help Karen decide what to do about Mr. Blackhawk if he comes around again. Since she won't let Emma file for a restraining order, does anybody have any other ideas?"

"Like I said earlier, speaking personally, that man gives me plenty of ideas," Emma said. "He's a hottie."

They all stared at her.

"A *hottie?*" Karen echoed incredulously.

"Are you denying it?" Emma asked.

"No, I'm trying to figure out how such a term became part of your Harvard-educated vernacular."

"Lauren," Emma said succinctly. "She spent all last night telling me which Hollywood leading men were really hotties and which ones weren't. It was quite an illuminating conversation. It set my heart aflutter, I'll tell you that."

"Oh, really?" Karen said. "Do you think maybe you've been single and celibate a little too long now? Maybe it's time to start looking for a replacement for your despicable ex-husband—or at least a hot date for Saturday night."

"I'm a single mom," Emma reminded her. "I don't have 'hot dates.'"

"Then look for something more serious," Karen advised. "I'm sure Caitlyn would be delighted to have a stepdaddy around, especially one who actually pays some attention to her."

"I think our friend here already found somebody," Cassie said, giving Emma a sly look.

"Don't be ridiculous. I have not," Emma protested.

"I don't know," Cassie countered. "I've seen you and the local newspaper editor with your heads together an awful lot lately. The two of you are in Stella's almost as much as I am, and I work there."

"And you know why that is," Emma said tightly. "It's about the case I'm working on. That's it. There is nothing personal involved."

"Protesting too much?" Cassie said, gazing around at the rest of them.

"Definitely," they chorused.

"Well, get over it," Emma snapped, gathering up her purse, her coat and her briefcase in a sudden rush. "I have to go."

She took a few steps across the room, then came back for the cell phone that was never more than an arm's length away. Then she swept out before any of them could react.

"Was it something we said?" Karen asked, staring after her.

"I think we hit the nail on the head," Cassie said, her expression thoughtful. "Wouldn't it be great if Emma did fall madly in love with Ford Hamilton or someone else in Winding River?"

"Just because you're married now doesn't mean that the rest of us have to jump into relationships," Gina pointed out.

"This isn't about having a relationship, though I think it would be great if she did," Cassie said. "It's just that I dread seeing Emma go back to Denver when this case here is over. She's been more relaxed the last few months, despite all of the commuting back and forth to Denver and the pressure of the trial coming up.''

"That's true," Lauren agreed. "She almost forgot her cell phone tonight. For a while last summer I thought it was attached to her hand."

They all fell silent as they considered Emma's welfare. It would be nice if she stayed, Karen thought. In fact, about the only thing good to come out of their high school reunion was that the five of them were spending more time in Wyoming again. She had missed having a tight-knit circle of friends more than she'd realized. And now, with Caleb gone, she treasured the friendships more than ever.

"Thank you for coming all the way over here tonight," she told them. "I don't know what I would have done without you these past few months. Every time I've been ready to come unglued, you've been here."

"And we'll continue to be here whenever you need us," Lauren said. "You can count on it."

That made two things today she could count on, Karen thought—her friends, and Grady Blackhawk's threat that he would be back time and again until she gave up and sold him the land he wanted.

Maybe it was all of Emma's talk about Grady's undeniable sex appeal, but that threat wasn't striking fear into her the way it should have, not the way it had just this afternoon. In fact, to her very deep regret, she was beginning to feel just the slightest hint of anticipation.

Chapter Three

Without even setting foot out of bed in the morning, Karen knew she was going to get up on the wrong side of it. Thanks to Emma, she had spent the whole night trying unsuccessfully to chase Grady Blackhawk out of her dreams. She'd awakened hot and restless, amid a tangle of sheets. She'd been feeling guilty to boot, all over sins her subconscious had committed in her sleep.

"I can't be blamed for that," she muttered as she shivered in the icy air and hastily pulled on jeans and an old flannel shirt of Caleb's. She hugged the shirt tighter around herself as a reminder of the man who'd really counted for something in her life.

She'd been doing that a lot lately, wearing shirts left hanging in Caleb's closet. Not all of them still held his scent, but the feel of the soft, faded flannel comforted her. It reminded her of evenings spent snuggled in his lap in front of a fire. It was a secret she'd shared with no one, fearful that her friends would chastise her for not moving on, for not letting go. She knew she had to, and she would when the time was right.

Just not yet, she thought with a sigh.

Once she'd tugged on thick socks and her boots, she went downstairs and turned up the thermostat to take the chill out of the air while she made a pot of coffee. To save on fuel costs, she would turn it back down again when she went outside to do the chores. Maybe it would only save pennies, but pennies counted these days.

She poured herself a cup of coffee, then took a sip. She cupped the mug in her hands to savor the warmth, then gazed out the window over the sink, hoping to catch a glimpse of the sunrise, rather than the more typical gray winter mornings they'd been having lately.

Instead, what she saw was Grady, unloading things from the back of his truck, looking perfectly at home. The sight of the man, after all those disturbing dreams, struck Karen as an omen. And not for anything good, either. No, indeed. His arrival definitely meant trouble. In fact, it looked almost as if he'd come to stay, as if he'd decided to claim this place whether she agreed to it or not.

She snatched a heavy jacket off the hook by the door and stormed outside, determined to put a stop to whatever he was up to. She was so infuriated by his presumption that he could just waltz in here and take over, she was surprised steam didn't rise from her as she crossed the yard.

"Why are you here again?" she demanded, her

tone deliberately unfriendly. The time for politeness and feigned hospitality was past. "I thought I'd made myself clear yesterday. You're not welcome."

He barely stopped what he was doing long enough to glance at her. His gaze skimmed her over from head to toe, his lips curved into the beginnings of a smile, then his attention went right back to a stack of lumber he was pulling from the back of the fancy new four-by-four.

That truck, parked next to her dilapidated pickup, which was in serious need of a paint job and a tune-up, grated on her nerves almost as much as his attitude. The man seemed to be mocking her in every way he knew.

"I asked you a question," she snapped.

"I didn't mean to disturb you," he said without any real hint of regret. "Figured you'd be out checking on your stock by now. Saw a couple of fence posts down on my way in. I can get to those tomorrow."

She bristled at the thinly veiled criticism, as well as the suggestion that he'd be back again. In fact, it sounded suspiciously as if he intended to pretty much take over.

"The hands will be fixing the fence today," she said, wanting him to believe that she had all the help she required. "There's no need for you to trouble yourself."

He grinned. "It's no trouble. In fact, I have some spare time. I thought I'd help out with a few things around here," he said mildly. "I noticed your barn could use a little work."

In her opinion, he noticed too blasted much. It was

annoying. "My barn is *my* problem. I don't want you anywhere near it."

"The work needs doing, right?"

"Yes, but—"

"And I have the time."

"I don't want you here."

"Never throw a friendly offer back in a man's face. He might think you don't appreciate a neighborly gesture."

Karen knew there was nothing friendly about Grady's intentions. He was up to something. She could see it in his eyes. And it wasn't as if he lived right down the road. He lived in the next county, too far away for there to be anything the least bit neighborly about this gesture.

Before she could respond to his taunt, he'd turned his back on her and headed for the barn, where paint she hadn't bought and tools she'd never seen before waited. He stripped off his jacket as if the temperature were seventy, instead of thirty-seven, and went to work, leaving her to struggle with her indignation and her desire to touch those broad shoulders he'd put on display in her side yard. His flannel shirt was stretched taut over well-developed muscles, not hanging as Caleb's was on her.

"I can't afford to pay for all of this," she hollered after him.

He heaved what sounded like a resigned sigh and faced her. "Did I ask for money?"

"No, but I feel obligated to pay for any fixing up that goes on around here."

"Then you'll pay me something when you have it," he said as if it was of no concern to him when— or even if—she did. "This barn can't take another winter in the state it's in. It'll cost you a lot more to replace it if it falls apart than it will if I take care of a few simple repairs now."

His gaze locked with hers. "You know I'm right, Karen."

Hearing him say her name startled her. The day before and in their one prior meeting, he'd been careful to be formally polite, referring to her as "Mrs. Hanson" when he used any name at all. Today, using her first name, he made it sound as if he'd forgotten all about her relationship with Caleb, as if they were about to become friends. She shuddered at the prospect. She didn't need a friend who made her feel all quivery inside, a man who'd already stated quite clearly that he wanted things from her that she didn't intend to give. Sure, it was land he was after, not her body, but her erratically beating pulse didn't seem to know the difference.

"What I know is that you are presuming to intrude in my life, to take over and do things I haven't asked you to do. Why? So I'll be in your debt?"

"It's a gesture, nothing more," he insisted. "I just want you to see that I'm not the bad guy your husband made me out to be."

"If you're such a nice guy, then why won't you listen when I tell you that I don't want you here?"

"Because you don't really mean it. That's just your pride talking."

She scowled, because he was at least partially right. Her pride—along with some very sensible suspicions about Grady's motives—was forcing her to look a much-needed gift horse in the mouth.

"Oh, forget it," she mumbled. She clearly wasn't going to get rid of him, so she might as well let him do whatever he intended to do and get it over with. She'd just ignore him, pretend he wasn't there. She certainly had plenty of her own chores to do.

She stalked past him into the barn, fed and watered the horses, mucked out stalls, then saddled up Ginger, the horse she'd owned since she was a teenager.

"We're getting out of here, girl."

"Running away?" Grady inquired from just behind her, amusement threading through his voice.

"No, I'm going out to see if Dooley and Hank need any help."

"Lucky Dooley and Hank."

She frowned at the teasing. "What is that supposed to mean?"

"Just that I'd welcome your help, if you were to offer."

"This is *your* project, Mr. Blackhawk. You'll have to finish it on your own. If there's something you can't cope with, you can always leave."

His gaze locked with hers. "It's not a matter of coping. I'd just be glad of the company."

Goose bumps that had nothing to do with the chilly air rose on her skin. She turned away and concentrated on tightening the cinch on Ginger's saddle.

"I seem to make you nervous, Karen. Why is that?"

She frowned as she faced him. "You don't make me nervous, Mr. Blackhawk. You make me *mad*."

He chuckled at that.

"You find that amusing?" she asked indignantly.

His gaze settled on her mouth. "No," he said softly. "I find it promising. A woman with a temper is always more fascinating than one who's docile."

"I'm not doing any of this to provide you with

entertainment,'' she snapped, trying not to acknowledge that his words sent an unaccustomed thrill shivering down her spine and set her pulse to racing.

"I know," he said, his grin spreading. "That's what makes it so enjoyable."

Karen bit back a retort that would only have escalated the ridiculous debate and mounted Ginger. Stepping back, Grady touched a finger to the brim of his hat in a polite salute.

"Enjoy your ride."

"I intend to," she lied. She doubted she would enjoy anything as long as this impossible man was underfoot.

An hour later, though, after riding hard, then meeting up with Hank and Dooley to check their progress on the fence repairs, she was feeling more at ease. She expected that to change the minute she reached the barn, but to her surprise Grady was nowhere in sight. His truck was gone, too. The sigh that eased through her was tinged with something she couldn't identify. Surely not regret, she thought with exasperation. No, it was relief, nothing more.

Unfortunately, though, her relief didn't last long. The evidence of Grady's presence and of his anticipated return was everywhere. The tools, paint cans and lumber were right where he'd left them. The ladder was still propped against the side of the barn, and the paint had been scraped only from the highest boards, with plenty left untouched.

She had barely cooled Ginger down and started for the house when his truck appeared in the distance, an unmistakable splash of red against the dull winter landscape. Karen hurried inside to avoid another pointless confrontation.

But as the afternoon wore on and her gaze kept straying to the man who was diligently and methodically stripping the old paint off her barn, she sighed and accepted the fact that he wasn't going to go away. She had to find some way to make peace with him.

In her experience, home-baked cookies were generally an excellent peace offering. With nobody around to appreciate the results, she hadn't had the urge to bake for some time now. Still, as a gesture of loyalty to her late husband, she made a deliberate choice to bake oatmeal-raisin cookies, her father's favorites, rather than the chocolate chip that Caleb had loved.

When the first batch was still warm from the oven, she put some of the cookies on a plate, poured a mug of coffee and carried it all across the yard. As she walked toward Grady, she could feel his speculative gaze burning into her.

The gesture had been a mistake, she concluded as she met his eyes. He was going to make too much of it, twist it somehow and use it as an opening. Impatient with herself for allowing room for him to jump to a conclusion that a truce was in the offing, she plunked coffee and plate down ungraciously and scurried back to the house.

She was all too aware that Grady's intent gaze followed her every step.

"You are such a ninny, Karen Hanson," she chided herself as she slammed the door behind her. "Taking the man a few cookies was polite. It wasn't an overture that he could misinterpret."

But despite the reassuring words, she was very much afraid that he had. And who knew where that would lead?

* * *

Grady was satisfied with the way the day had gone. He'd made progress. At least Karen hadn't thrown him off the property. In fact, she'd baked him cookies, as if he were a schoolboy who deserved nourishment for doing a chore.

She'd regretted it, too. He'd seen that in her eyes and in the way she'd retreated to the house with such haste that he hadn't even had time to thank her.

One of these days they might actually sit down and have a real conversation, he mused. After that, who knew what might be accomplished? Maybe she would listen to reason.

Of course, in his experience, women were emotional creatures. Reason didn't matter half as much to them as it did to men. Which meant he would just have to appeal to Karen's heart. How he was supposed to do that when it was her heart that was telling her to throw his offer back in his face was beyond him, but he would figure it out. He was too close to his goal now to let anything stand in his way.

Grady figured he had another week's work on the barn. Then he'd move on to something else. And something else after that, if need be. He considered the time and money an investment. After all, the work needed to be done anyway and the property would be his someday soon.

Grady leaned against the rung of the ladder and munched on the last cookie. He hadn't had a decent oatmeal-raisin cookie in years, not since one of his classmates had moved away in sixth grade. Luke's mama had baked the best oatmeal-raisin cookies ever. None he'd tried in all the years since had lived up to them…until now.

He stared toward the house, saw a light come on in the kitchen and knew she was in there fixing supper. Did she cook for herself now that Caleb was gone? Or did she put together a careless snack, a sandwich maybe, or even nothing more than a bowl of cold cereal and milk? That's what he found himself doing more nights than not. It didn't seem worth the effort to fix a hearty meal. When his body demanded something substantial, he drove into town and ate out. He'd become a regular at Stella's, ignoring the fact that Cassie Davis tended to regard him with suspicion much of the time. If she should consider the entrée he'd gained into Karen's life an intrusion, he might have to check his supper for arsenic.

Staring over at the house, he felt nagged by curiosity until he convinced himself that going to the door to return his mug and give Karen a proper thanks for those cookies was the gentlemanly thing to do.

As he tapped on the glass, he could see her shadowy movements inside, saw her go still, hesitate, then finally move toward the door. He could imagine her sigh of resignation as she crossed the kitchen.

"Yes?" she said, her tone surly, her expression forbidding.

Grady saw past that, though, to the hint of loneliness in her eyes. Of course, her irritation was doing a mighty fine job of covering it up, but he'd caught a glimpse of it just the same. Or maybe that was just an excuse to prolong the encounter.

He held out the mug and the plate. "Just wanted to thank you for the coffee and the cookies."

"You're welcome," she said, taking the dishes and already starting to shut the door in his face.

He blocked it with the toe of his boot. He was

about to do something he was likely to regret, but he couldn't seem to stop himself.

"What are you doing for supper, Karen?"

Her gaze narrowed. "Why? Are you inviting yourself?"

He grinned. "Not at all. My mama taught me better manners than that. I was going to invite you to join me over in Winding River. I'm partial to Stella's meat loaf, and that's the special tonight. I hate to eat alone."

She was shaking her head before the words were out of his mouth. "I couldn't."

"Don't want to be seen with me?" he challenged.

"That's not it," she said with a touch of impatience. "I've already started fixing my own supper. It would go to waste."

"I don't suppose there's enough for two?" he asked hopefully.

A smile tugged at the corners of her mouth. "Have you forgotten your manners so soon, Mr. Blackhawk?"

"Like I said, I hate to eat alone. I think my mama would forgive me just this once for being pushy. How about you? Can you forgive me? Maybe take pity on a poor bachelor who rarely gets a homecooked meal?"

"Oh, for heaven's sakes, come on in," she said with a shake of her head. "You're impossible, Mr. Blackhawk."

Grady hid a grin as he entered. He hung his hat and jacket on a peg by the door, then sniffed the air. "Why, I do believe you're making meat loaf."

"Which I'm sure you knew before you made that

outrageous claim about it being one of your favorites."

Grady didn't deny it. Instead, he looked around and asked, "What can I do? Want me to set the table, or are you afraid I'll steal the silver?"

"No silver," she said. "I think I can trust you with the stainless-steel utensils and the everyday dishes. You don't strike me as a clumsy man."

"I try not to be...especially when there's a beautiful woman watching."

She flushed at that, but in less than a heartbeat, her eyes flashed sparks. "Don't try flattering me, Mr. Blackhawk."

He frowned. "Can we get past the formalities? I've been calling you Karen all day long. Can't you call me Grady?"

He saw her struggle reflected on her face, knew that she considered it one step closer to an intimacy she didn't want. She was too polite to tell him that, though. She merely nodded curtly.

"Grady, then."

"Thank you," he said, keeping his expression and his tone deliberately solemn.

"Are you mocking me?"

"Not mocking," he said. "Just teasing a little."

"Well, I don't like it," she said sharply.

"Oh, really? When was the last time a man teased you, Karen?"

"I'm sure you know the answer to that."

"When Caleb was still alive," he suggested. "Tell me about him."

She stared at him with surprise written all over her face. "Why?"

"Because I'd like to know how you saw him. I

imagine it was quite a bit different from the way *I* viewed him.''

''Yes, I imagine it was,'' she replied wryly. ''He was my husband and I loved him.''

''Needless to say, I didn't. He always struck me as an unreasonable man, one who twisted the facts to suit himself,'' Grady said, deliberately baiting her just to see the flash of fire in her eyes, the color blooming in her cheeks. He liked seeing her come alive, instead of wearing the defeated air he'd seen on his arrival the day before.

''Caleb was the fairest men I ever knew,'' she retorted, her voice as prickly as a desert cactus. ''Which is why I owe it to him to think twice before I believe a word you say. You tell me you weren't responsible for any of those incidents that almost cost us our herd, but words aren't evidence. Where's your proof?''

He leveled a look straight into her soft blue eyes. ''Where's yours?''

She swallowed hard at that and turned away, dishing up mashed potatoes, gravy and meat loaf with quick, impatient gestures that told him his barb had gotten to her.

Silently she slapped a fresh loaf of country sourdough bread on the table, along with home-churned butter, then took a seat opposite him.

''Shall we call a truce, Karen?'' he suggested mildly. ''Otherwise, we're going to ruin a perfectly fine meal, and we'll both end up with indigestion.''

''Calling a truce with you is a risk,'' she said candidly. ''You tend to take advantage every chance you get.''

''I'm highly motivated. Is there anything wrong with that?''

"I suppose that depends on your motivation and your goal."

"You know mine. I've laid all my cards on the table. What about you? What motivates you?" He noticed that the travel brochures had been gathered up and tossed into a basket on the counter. "Dreams of faraway places?"

"Dreams can be a motivation," she conceded, though it wasn't a direct answer to his question. Her gaze met his. "Or merely a fantasy."

"Which are they for you?"

"Fantasy at the moment, nothing more."

She was fibbing, he decided, noting that the brochure for London was already dog-eared from handling.

"If you could go anywhere in the world you wanted, where would you choose?"

"London," she said at once, then seemed to regret it.

"Any particular reason?"

"Lots of them, but I'm sure you'd find then all boring."

"I wouldn't have asked if I didn't want to know."

She hesitated, then shrugged as if to concede his point. "I studied literature the one year I went away to college. I love Jane Austen and Charles Dickens and Thackery. I love Shakespeare's sonnets. And for me, London is permeated with the spirit of all the great British authors. Some of them are even buried in Westminster Abbey."

"You're a romantic," Grady concluded.

"You say that as if it's a crime."

"No, just a surprise. Romantics don't always do

well in the real world. Ranching can be a hard life. There's very little romantic about it.''

She gave him a pitying look. ''Then you've been doing it with the wrong person. I found my share of romance right here.''

''Is that why you don't want to leave? Nostalgia?''

''You already know why I won't sell this ranch—at least not to you.''

Rather than heading down that particular dead-end road again right now, Grady concentrated on his meal for a moment. ''You're a fine cook,'' he said as he ate the last bite of meat loaf on his plate.

''Thank you.''

''You'll have to let me return the favor sometime. Not that I'll cook, but I'd be happy to take you out for supper.''

''I don't think so, but thank you for offering.''

That stiff, polite tone was back in her voice. Grady couldn't help wondering what it would be like to see her defenses slip, to hear her laugh.

Whether that ever happened or not wasn't important, he chided himself. He only needed her to trust him just a little, to persuade her that she wasn't cut out for the life of a rancher. And then to coax her into selling this land to him and not someone else.

He shoved his chair back and stood up. ''Thanks for the meal. I'll see you in the morning.''

She seemed startled. ''No angling for dessert?''

''Not tonight,'' he said, then hesitated. ''Unless you've got an apple pie warming in the oven.''

She shook her head, amusement brightening her eyes. ''No, just more oatmeal cookies.''

He considered that but concluded, good as they were, he didn't dare risk staying. Sitting here with lovely Karen Hanson in her kitchen was entirely too cozy.

"I wouldn't mind taking one or two along for the drive," he said.

"After my cookies, then, and not my company? Should I be insulted?" she asked, but she put a few into a bag for him.

"I'll leave that to you," he said, giving her a wink that clearly disconcerted her. "See you in the morning."

"Yes," she said with what sounded like resignation. "I imagine you will."

Grady closed the door quietly, then stood on the other side feeling a bit disconcerted himself. He was already looking forward to morning, and that wasn't good. It wasn't good at all, because he knew that this time it had less to do with the land and more to do with the woman who was keeping it from him. And that hadn't been part of his plan at all.

Chapter Four

Karen woke before dawn, did the necessary chores, left a note in the barn for Pete and Dooley and high-tailed it away from the ranch. She headed straight for Winding River, though she didn't have a specific destination in mind.

Okay, so what if she was running away? She had a right to, didn't she? Her home wasn't her own anymore, not with Grady evidently intending to pop up like a stubborn weed every time she turned around.

Sitting across the kitchen table from him the night before had rattled her more than she liked. Other than inflicting his presence on her in the sneakiest way possible, he hadn't been the least bit pushy. The subject of the ranch had hardly arisen at all.

Instead, he had been attentive and lighthearted. The conversation had been intelligent. All in all, he had been very good company. He'd flattered her some, reminding her that it was nice to receive a compliment from a man every now and again.

Just not from *this* man, she scolded herself. Nothing out of Grady's mouth could be trusted. It was all a means to an end, and that end was taking the Hanson ranch away from her, whether he actually mentioned his desire to buy the place or not.

Funny, that was how she thought of the ranch, not so much as her own but as still belonging to the Hansons, with her merely its guardian. These days the duty was weighing heavily on her shoulders.

A pale, shimmery sun was trying to sneak over the horizon as she drove onto Main Street in Winding River and headed straight for Stella's. Not only would the coffee be hot, but Cassie was likely to be working. Cole had chafed at her decision to stay on after the wedding, but Cassie had been insistent. In Karen's opinion, even now, with things between Cassie and Cole improving and Jake thrilled to be living with his long-lost dad, her old friend didn't trust that the marriage was going to last. Cassie wanted the security of her own money and a familiar job. Since Cole worked at home, he was there when nine-year-old Jake got home each day, but even if he hadn't been, Cassie would have found a way to remain independent.

"My gracious, you must have been up with the birds," Stella greeted her when Karen walked through the door.

"Before most of them," Karen said.

"Something on your mind?" the woman asked as she poured coffee and set the cup in front of her. "Won't be anybody else in here for a few minutes yet. I could listen."

Karen hesitated, then nodded. "If you wouldn't mind."

Stella sat down across from her. She had known all five of the Calamity Janes since they were in grade school, which was when she'd first opened the restaurant. With her ready smile, huge heart and nonjudgmental demeanor, Stella had been mother and friend and mentor to all of them at one time or another. She was playing the same role for another generation now.

"Okay, what is it?" Stella probed. "You still grieving over Caleb?"

"Yes, of course," Karen said a little too hastily, as if she had something to prove. "He's only been gone a little over half a year."

Stella's gaze narrowed. "The way you said that, all defensive when I just asked a simple question...it's another man, isn't it? You're attracted to someone and you're feeling guilty?"

"No," Karen denied heatedly, then flinched under Stella's steady gaze. "Okay, maybe. It's just that there's this man who wants the ranch. He's been pestering me."

"Grady Blackhawk," Stella said at once. "I've heard all about it."

"From Cassie, I imagine."

"From her and from Grady himself. He comes in here from time to time."

Karen thought of their conversation the night before. "For the meat loaf?"

Stella grinned. "That man does love my meat loaf. Of course, he's also partial to chicken-fried steak and pot roast. Any man who drives as far as he does for my food is either close to starving or he genuinely likes it.''

"You sound as if you approve of him.''

"I do,'' Stella said, regarding Karen closely. "Why does that surprise you?'' She held up a hand. "Never mind. I know. It's because there was bad blood between him and Caleb.''

"Can you think of a better reason?''

"Sure. One that you came up with on your own after giving the man a chance.'' She studied Karen gravely. "I think maybe that's what's bothering you. You're kind by nature. You give most people a fair chance to prove themselves. A second chance when it's called for. You're not doing that with Grady, and it doesn't sit well with you.''

"Maybe that's right,'' Karen admitted. It was true that she liked to form her own opinions about people. And she'd never taken the view that a husband and wife had to have the exact same friends—so why was she so determined to make Caleb's enemy into her own?

Because Caleb was dead, of course. Who would stand up to Grady if she didn't do it? And it wasn't about personalities, anyway. It was about the ranch.

"Are you going to sell the ranch to Grady?'' Stella asked, getting to the point.

"No,'' Karen said.

"Then what's the problem? Sounds to me as if your decision is made and it's final.''

"He…'' She regarded Stella with the helpless feeling of a teenager admitting to a crush. After a minute, she gathered her courage and said it. "Grady bothers me.'' It felt surprisingly good to get the words out, words she hadn't been able to manage to her oldest friends, even when they'd given her ample opportunity to say them.

A grin tugged at Stella's lips. She didn't look the least bit shocked. "Is that so? Now, if you ask me, you've just admitted to being a full-fledged, red-blooded female. That man is something to look at. Ain't a woman living who would deny feeling her senses go into overdrive when he walks into a room."

"Really?" Karen asked hopefully. "Then I'm not being disloyal to Caleb's memory?"

"Sweetie, I would tell you the same thing if Caleb were still alive and sitting right here across from you. There's not a thing wrong with looking at a fine specimen of a man. Now *doing something about it* is a whole other story." Her gaze narrowed. "You thinking of getting involved with Grady? Is that the way things are moving?"

"Absolutely not," Karen said fiercely. She had never allowed her thoughts to stray beyond admitting to an attraction. And she wouldn't permit herself to go any further.

Stella chuckled. "Then you might want to temper that protest just a little. Sounds a little too emphatic, if you know what I mean."

Unfortunately, Karen knew exactly what she meant. "I'm in trouble, aren't I?"

"Not yet, but you could be looking at it," the older woman said. She reached across the table and patted Karen's hand. "And to tell the truth, I don't think that would be such a bad thing. There's no set timetable for grieving, not like in the old days, when people were expected to put everything on hold for a full year of mourning. Life goes on, Karen. It's meant for living. Caleb wouldn't begrudge you happiness. Just be sure the timing is right for *you,* not Grady."

"It's wrong," she said, as much to herself as to Stella. "Caleb hated him."

Stella gave her a serious look. "Meaning no disrespect to your husband—he was a good boy and a fine man—but he held on to grudges that weren't his. Don't you do the same."

Before Karen could ask what Stella had meant by grudges that weren't Caleb's, the door opened and the first rush of morning customers came in, bringing cold air and shouted pleas for hot coffee with them.

"Just think about what I've said," Stella said as she stood up. "I'll bring you your breakfast in a minute. Let me get these heathens settled down first."

"I haven't ordered," Karen pointed out.

"No need. You have the same thing every time, the number three with the egg scrambled."

As Stella walked away, Karen thought about that, thought about everything going on in her life. "I'm in a rut," she muttered, just as Cassie slid into the booth opposite her.

"Talking to yourself is not a good sign," she advised Karen. "I only have a second before it gets crazy in here. Are you okay? Need somebody to talk to?"

"I did, but Stella filled in."

Cassie grinned. "She always has. Now sit tight. I imagine Emma will be in shortly to keep you company. Of course, Ford may be right behind her. The man's been like her shadow lately. She still says it's wearing on her nerves, but she hasn't chased him off yet. What about you? Did you chase Grady Blackhawk off permanently the other day?"

"Afraid not," Karen admitted ruefully. "In fact, that's why I'm here. He was at the ranch all day yesterday and said he'd be back today."

Cassie's expression turned indignant. "All day? What is wrong with that man? He wasn't pressuring you again, was he? Maybe Emma was right about getting a restraining order."

"No, he wasn't pressuring me, not the way you mean. In fact, just the opposite. He showed up and went straight to work without a word to me. When I caught sight of him, he was stripping the paint off the barn."

Cassie looked as stunned as Karen had felt when she'd first seen him outside. "What? Why would he do a thing like that?"

"Your guess is as good as mine," she said wearily. "He seems to have a list of projects he intends to help me with. Did I ask for that help? No. Do I want it? No. Does he listen to a word I say? No."

Her friend chuckled. "Interesting. A man who can't take no for an answer. I have one at home just like that."

"Don't even go there," Karen said.

Before the morning was out, she had advice from Emma and Gina and Lauren, all of whom had popped in and out of Stella's just long enough to grab some food before getting on with their days. Unfortunately, the only way Karen could get on with her day or her life would be to go home…where Grady would be waiting.

Since she was not prepared to deal with the man— or her own tangled emotions—again so soon, she headed for Laramie instead. Maybe a movie and some wistful window-shopping—the only kind of shopping she could afford right now—would get her mind off him. At the very least, it would mean she could delay dealing with Grady until tomorrow.

Unfortunately, the lead in the movie she chose looked a lot like Grady. And the actor who resembled her sexy nemesis was the romantic hero, not the villain. It seemed that everything was conspiring to change her opinion of Grady, which meant she was just going to have to cling more tightly to all the warnings Caleb had uttered over the years. Maybe, if she repeated them like a mantra, this uneasy weakening of her resolve would end, and she could go on with her life as before.

True, these days everything seemed a bit rocky and difficult, but she'd take that anytime over dealing with Grady and the unlikely, inappropriate feelings he'd begun to stir in her.

Grady didn't bother going to the door when he arrived the next day. He just started to work, counting on Karen to spot him sooner or later as she had the day before. He couldn't seem to stop his gaze from drifting to the house now and again, though, as he tried to imagine what Karen was up to inside.

Was she baking again? Those cookies had been the best he'd had in a long time. He couldn't help wondering if there were any left or when she might appear with a few. Or maybe she'd taken the hint about an apple pie. Maybe one was cooling on top of the stove right now. He'd been on his own so long that the mere thought of home-baked treats made his mouth water.

Fortunately, he'd learned never to rely on wishful thinking when it came to food or drink. He'd brought a thermos filled with coffee and a cooler with him.

The latter was filled with sandwiches and sodas, enough to share in that warm, cozy kitchen if the opportunity arose. He didn't like the stirring of disappointment he felt when noon came and went with no sign of the woman with whom he'd meant to enjoy his meal.

So far the only company he'd had were the two part-time hands, who regarded him with suspicion when they found him atop a ladder scraping the last of the paint off the side of the barn.

"Who're you?" the grizzled older man had demanded within a few minutes of Grady's arrival.

"Grady Blackhawk," he replied, keeping his temper in check at their obviously dismayed reaction to his name. "And you?"

"Ain't none of your business who we are. We belong here and you don't. What are you doing on Hanson property and makin' yourself right at home, at that?"

"Isn't that obvious?"

"Not to me it ain't," the old man said. "No way Mrs. Hanson would let you come sniffin' around here, much less approve of you bein' out here messin' with her barn."

"And why is that?" he asked, curious to see what Karen might have said about him.

"Because now that her husband's dead and buried, you're trying to steal this place right out from under her," the younger man said. He gestured toward the paint cans stacked nearby in readiness for the next step in Grady's project. "You trying to work up a debt she won't be able to pay off?"

"Absolutely not," Grady insisted. "I'm just doing her a favor."

"Now why would you do that, unless you had somethin' up your sleeve?" the old man asked. "Nobody does somethin' for nothin'."

"Is that a fact?" Grady asked mildly. "Well, in this case, you're wrong. I'm just being neighborly."

"Humph!" the old man said with a snort of disbelief. "Good thing she ain't around to see this. Woman has enough on her mind without seein' you out here makin' like you have a right to be here."

"Karen's not home?" he said, barely concealing his disappointment.

"That's Mrs. Hanson to you," the old man retorted. "And no, she ain't here. So if you were hopin' to annoy her, you're plumb out of luck. She's gone for the day. Maybe longer, for all I know. Could be gone weeks. Maybe she finally went off on that fancy vacation her friends have been urgin' her to take."

Grady concluded the exaggeration was meant for his benefit. He should have seen for himself that she wasn't around. That heap of hers was gone. Maybe he'd just been hoping someone had come and towed it off to the junkyard where it belonged.

"Seriously," he said, "did she say when she'll be back?"

The two men exchanged a look, then the older one shook his head with obvious reluctance. "Not to me, she didn't."

"Me, either," the younger one said.

"I imagine she did leave you with chores to do, though, didn't she?" Grady said pointedly.

"That she did," the old man agreed.

Even so, for a minute Grady thought they might stand right there for the rest of the day to keep an eye on him. But eventually their sense of duty overcame their suspicions and they wandered away, the old man still muttering under his breath about the nerve of some people.

Ironically, Grady was actually relieved by their reaction. It meant there were people looking out for Karen, people who had her best interests at heart, even if they were sadly misguided where he was concerned.

Or maybe not, he thought wryly. Maybe they had it just right. His intentions weren't quite as honorable as he'd made them out to be. It would be wise if all of them remembered that, himself included.

He went back to work, contenting himself with the progress he was making in scraping off the old paint. That was why he'd come, after all. He wasn't here to see Karen Hanson with her big blue, vulnerable eyes and kissable lips.

And pigs flew, he thought with a sigh as his gaze strayed time and again toward the driveway where he hoped to catch a glimpse of her beat-up old truck kicking up a plume of dust.

But as night fell, there was still no sign of Karen. Even though the two men had told him she'd gone out, Grady knocked on the door in case they'd merely been trying to throw him off, but there was no answer. No welcoming lights came on in the kitchen as it grew darker.

He poured himself a last cup of coffee from his thermos and settled into the shadows of the front porch to wait for her return. He was grateful for his sheepskin-lined jacket as the air turned cold. There was the scent of snow in it, though a blizzard hadn't been predicted before the following week.

As the minutes ticked by, he was tempted to throw

in the towel and leave, but he stayed right where he was. He couldn't explain why he was so determined to hang around until Karen's return. He felt sure he wouldn't like the answer if he tried.

When Karen drove up at last, the headlights cut through the darkness, clearly outlining him in the rocker. She turned off the pickup's engine, but she didn't emerge. He could just imagine her sitting there, battling irritation...or maybe even temptation. Was she struggling with it the same way he was?

When she finally stepped from the car, slammed the door and headed his way with a brisk stride, he concluded irritation had won. He stood to meet her, eager for a battle that was bound to warm the air by several degrees.

"What are you doing here at this hour?" she asked mildly enough. "You're too far away from the barn to claim you're painting."

"I was waiting for you. You were out late for a woman with so much work to do around here," he said mildly.

"I thought *you'd* taken over all the hard chores," she tossed back. "So I figured I could take a day off," she added cheerfully.

"Is that it? My guess is you were hiding out. Surely, I don't scare you, do I?"

"Don't be ridiculous. You annoy me, you don't scare me. On top of that, my comings and goings are no concern of yours," she declared with an expected flash of temper that virtually heated the chilly night air.

He concluded that he'd hit the nail on the head. She'd stayed away today to avoid him and was thoroughly exasperated that the tactic had failed.

"A lady can never have too many people worrying about her," he said. "Not in this day and age."

She stuffed her hands into her pockets and met his gaze evenly. "Would it surprise you to know that the only thing in my life my friends are concerned about is *you?*"

Grady felt his lips twitch. "Not a bit. I imagine you've painted a pretty dark picture of me. Your two hands certainly seemed suspicious enough when they found me here."

"I imagine they were. Dooley and Hank were very loyal to Caleb. They look out for me."

"There's no need to worry about me. I'm not such a bad guy," he asserted.

"Couldn't prove it by me."

"You realize, of course, that you don't know me at all," he reminded her yet again.

"I know enough."

He took a step closer, admiring the fact that she didn't back away. "Such as?"

"You're a scoundrel and a thief," she said flatly, dredging up old news.

Even though they'd been over this ground before, it was evident she intended to cling to that description. Maybe it was what she used to battle the undeniable sparks of attraction zinging between them even now.

He stepped closer, deliberately crowding her. She continued to stand her ground, though there was an unmistakable flash of alarm in her eyes. "Really?" he said softly. "You know that for a fact?"

"My husband said—"

He lifted his hand and brushed a wayward strand of hair away from her cheek, felt her skin heat. "Yes, you've quoted him before," he said, pulling away before the gesture could turn into a caress. "But what do you know, Karen? Not rumor. Not innuendo. Pure fact."

In the light of a pale half-moon, he could see her throat work as she struggled with the possibility that she had judged him unfairly. It was clear she didn't have an answer for him, and just as clear that she didn't like that about herself.

"I'll make you a deal," he said in the same coaxing tone he'd use to gentle a wild horse. "You get to know me. Spend time with me. If you still think I'm a scoundrel and a thief, I'll walk away and not bother you about the land again. If I prove otherwise, you'll sell the ranch to me and get on with that traveling you've always dreamed about."

"I can't," she said, her voice a little breathless.

"Why not? Don't you trust your own judgment?"

"Of course, but—"

"It's a fair deal, Karen. You know it is."

"I still can't do it," she said.

She said it flatly, but Grady thought there was a slightly wistful note in her voice for the first time.

"Suit yourself. I'll just come up with some other way to go about this," he said with an indifferent shrug, and started to walk away. He didn't get far.

"This experiment of yours," she called after him, sounding resigned. "How long would it last and what would it entail?"

He turned back to face her. "As long as it takes and whatever's necessary."

She shook her head. "Absolutely not. It'll only work if there are rules and we both agree to them."

"Okay, then," he relented. "A month and we'll

only share a few meals, a little conversation. Nothing more. What's the harm in that? We got through dinner last night without the world coming to an end, didn't we?''

"I suppose."

"So, what do you say? Is it a deal?"

"Two weeks," she countered, her defiant gaze locked with his.

"Two weeks," he agreed, seizing it. He bit back his desire to utter a whoop of triumph. "Lunch and dinner."

"You'll be satisfied with that?" she asked, gaze narrowed as she studied him. "Whatever my decision at the end of two weeks, you'll live with it? You'll accept it if I say you haven't convinced me of anything?"

"That's the agreement."

She held out her hand. Grady clasped it, felt her tremble, and knew he'd just made the smartest deal of his life.

As he walked away, he murmured under his breath, "Two weeks is a start, darlin'. That's a real good start."

Chapter Five

*W*hat had she done? Karen rested her head on her arms and groaned as she considered Grady's trap and the way she'd neatly stepped into it with virtually no hesitation at all. She had invited the enemy into the camp and promised to break bread with him. She had to be out of her mind.

But somehow, in the quiet stillness of the night, she hadn't been able to resist what he was offering— a chance to end this battle once and for all.

More, it was a chance to unravel a puzzle that was increasingly complex. Why she cared so much about that didn't bear thinking about. She feared it went beyond fair play, beyond curiosity. In fact, she had a terrible sense that it had to do with a yearning that had started in the pit of her stomach and hadn't let up since the day he'd appeared in her kitchen.

It could be as simple as a yearning for companion-

ship, something she'd missed desperately in the
weeks and months since Caleb's death. A worrisome
voice in the back of her mind told her it was something more, something specific to Grady, the allure of
the forbidden.

She hadn't been the rule-breaker all those years
ago. That had been Cassie. But, oh, how Karen had
longed to be just like her, to shake things up, defy
convention. Spending time with Grady would certainly qualify. There would be talk. Her in-laws were
likely to be outraged. Deep down, even she disapproved of the choice she had made.

But it was done now. She couldn't go back on her
word. It was only a few meals, she reminded herself.
How difficult could that be? How much trouble could
she get into by spending an occasional hour in
Grady's company?

She found out when lunch turned out to be a daily
ritual and dinner slipped into the schedule six nights
out of seven. By the end of the first week of their
agreement, she'd almost grown comfortable having
Grady around. She'd almost forgotten why he was
there. The wicked danger of it all faded when he continued to behave like a perfect gentleman.

Then came the Saturday night that snow started
falling while they were sharing a meal of beef stew
and homemade bread. Karen wasn't aware that the
weather had changed outside as Grady beguiled her
with stories of his grandfather.

As the tales unfolded, it became evident that
Thomas Blackhawk was an amazing man, one who
fought to preserve his Native American heritage while
getting along quite well in a white man's world. He

was mayor of his town in the northwest part of the state and there was some talk that he might run for a position as delegate from the region to the state legislature.

"The first time I ever saw him dressed in a suit and tie, I couldn't believe it was him," Grady said, his eyes twinkling. "I'd seen him most often in jeans and flannel, but there he was speaking to a crowd at a town meeting, wearing this fancy black suit, his lined face filled with pride. It was quite a transformation. When I commented on it afterward, do you know what he said?"

"What?" Karen asked, fascinated.

"That all the fancy clothes in the world couldn't make a man respect you. It was actions that did that."

"You love him a lot, don't you?"

"It's more than that," Grady said. "I love him and I admire him. He lives a very simple life in the middle of nowhere, in a house he built himself. As a kid I spent a lot of time with him, listening to him talk about nature, about our place in the universe. He taught me all of the old legends and practices, but those weren't the most important lessons, by far."

"What were the really important ones?" Karen asked.

"He taught me about self-respect and loyalty, about family and duty."

She thought she saw where this was going. "Was he the one who taught you to hate the Hansons?"

"Not to hate them," Grady denied. "My grandfather has never hated anyone. He just made me aware that this land should have belonged to his father, that it should have been Blackhawk land."

"In other words, he planted a seed in your head,

watered it regularly and now it's grown into this obsession,'' she said, derision cutting into the admiration she had begun to feel for Thomas Blackhawk.

''It's not an obsession, Karen. It's a commitment.
I want my grandfather to stand on this land someday,
look around and know that it's back with its rightful
owners, that it's Blackhawk land again.''

''Would he be happy about that if he knew the
price you'd paid?'' she asked.

''Dollars aren't the issue,'' he told her.

''No,'' she agreed. ''And I wasn't talking about the
amount of money you say you're willing to put on
the table. I was talking about the rest, the attempts
you've made to force Caleb, and now me, to sell.''

He regarded her with obvious impatience. ''Dammit, I've told you I had nothing to do with trying to
sabotage your herd.''

''If not you, who?''

''Both things could have been accidents. Cattle get
ill. Pastures catch on fire during a dry summer.''

She regarded him evenly. ''Do you honestly believe that's what happened? Isn't it a little too coin-
cidental that both the outbreak of disease and the fire
happened to our herd and no one else's?''

''I'll admit it looks suspicious, but I had nothing
to do with any of it.''

''So you say.''

''In a lot of very powerful circles, my word is good
enough.''

''All that tells me is that the world is filled with
foolish people,'' she said, stubbornly clinging to
her—no, Caleb's—conviction that Grady couldn't be
trusted. She needed these reminders from time to
time. Otherwise, it would be too easy to start to like

him a little too much, to begin to believe the pretty words that tripped so easily off his tongue.

He gave her a steady look, one clearly designed to rattle her. "Can you honestly sit there and look me in the eye and tell me that you think I'm capable of trying to destroy your herd just to get what I want? Have I done anything in the last week that was the least bit underhanded? Have I pressured you in any way?"

"No," she was forced to admit. Not unless the fact that he was here in the first place counted as a crime. The truth was he'd been helpful and considerate. He'd done everything in his power to ingratiate himself with her, tackling odd jobs too long ignored. The ranch buildings had never been in better condition.

"Well, then, shouldn't you be starting to trust me just a little?" he asked.

"I do," she conceded with a sigh, then met his gaze. "A little."

He grinned. "Another good start, darlin'. We're making progress."

Karen wasn't sure they were making the right kind of progress. She was absolutely certain Caleb wouldn't approve of it. She pushed away from the table, because it was becoming too tempting to linger, to share a second cup of coffee and a little more conversation each time they were together.

"I'd better get these dishes washed," she said, turning her back on him.

Grady was on his feet at once. "Let me help."

"No need," she insisted. "I'm sure you want to be heading home."

He grinned at that. "Not especially. The company's better right here. And it's Saturday night, a time to settle back and relax a little. I brought a video. I thought maybe we could make some popcorn and watch it together.''

The prospect was more alluring than she cared to admit. "Sorry," she said edgily. "No popcorn in the house.''

"I brought that, too.''

"You do think of everything, don't you?" she said in a way not meant to be complimentary.

"I try to," he agreed, not taking offense. "Shall I get the movie, or are you going to turn me down?''

She hesitated, then asked, "What movie is it?''

"One of Lauren's," he said with a smug expression. "It just came out on video.''

She frowned at him. "You knew I wouldn't be able to resist that, didn't you?''

"No, but I was hoping.''

The chances to get to Laramie for a movie had been too few and far between. The one she'd seen a week ago had been the first one since before Caleb's death. The last one of Lauren's she'd viewed in a theater had been a year ago. She told herself she was merely eager to catch up on her friend's career, not for the lingering company of the disconcerting man who'd brought the video.

"Get it," she told him. "I'll finish up here.''

Grady grabbed his jacket and opened the back door, allowing a blast of frigid air into the kitchen. When he shut it again without taking a step outside, Karen regarded him with curiosity.

"Anything wrong?" she asked.

"I suppose that depends on your point of view," he said with a wry note in his voice.

She crossed the room and opened the door to see

for herself. Great white flakes of snow were swirling around in blinding sheets. She could barely see the lighted outline of the barn in the distance. The ground had already been blanketed with a layer several inches thick. At this rate, the roads would be impassable in no time, if they weren't already.

Even as the implications of the blizzard sank in, she couldn't help being awed by the beauty of the snow-covered landscape. Rugged terrain softened and glistened.

She had learned long ago how to weather a storm. There were supplies on hand, a generator to keep the most basic electricity functioning and a well-stocked woodpile by the back door.

The only problem, of course, was the fact that she was going to be stuck here for who-knew-how-long with Grady. She couldn't send him out in this, not with the distance he'd have to drive. Maybe if he lived just up the road, they could have risked it, but he was miles from home.

The prospect of allowing him to stay under her roof didn't disconcert her nearly as much as it should have. This was an emergency. Who could make anything of it if he stayed? Who would even know?

She closed the door carefully, then announced briskly, "You'll stay here, of course. I'll go check the guest room and make sure you'll have everything you need."

"Karen," he said softly, drawing her attention.

"Yes?"

"I didn't plan this."

She allowed herself a brief smile at that. "No, I imagine not even *you* can control the weather."

"I didn't know it was predicted," he amended.

"Grady, I know enough about storms to know that they can come up unexpectedly, be worse than anticipated, any of that. I'm not thinking that you somehow conspired to find a way to spend the night here."

He nodded. "Okay, just so we're clear."

"We are," she said, amused despite herself. "Why don't you go ahead and get that movie and the popcorn?"

"If you're sure. I could still try to make it home."

"And wind up stranded in a snowdrift? I don't think so. I don't want that on my conscience."

"And we both know how worrisome you find that conscience of yours," he said lightly. "I'll get the movie. And I'll check on the stock in the barn to make sure there's plenty of feed."

"Thank you. Now go, before it gets any worse."

Only after he had gone outside did she sag against the kitchen counter. She had just invited Grady Blackhawk to stay in her home. The only thing the Hansons would consider a worse betrayal was if she'd invited him into her bed.

Grady trudged through the deepening snow to the barn and checked on the horses. It took no more than a few minutes, but by the time he went back outside, the house was lost behind a seemingly impenetrable wall of white. He found the guideline installed for occasions just like this and made his way slowly through drifts than were now knee-high and growing.

Thankfully his truck was parked close to the house. It took him several minutes to wipe the layer of snow from the door. The lock was frozen, but he always kept a de-icing tool in his pocket this time of year. Shivering, he got the door open, grabbed the video and popcorn, then closed the truck up and headed inside. He stomped the snow from his boots on the back steps, then removed his jacket and shook it off before stepping into the kitchen.

The heat felt like heaven to his stiff fingers. Not even gloves had been much protection against the falling temperature and wind. He was rubbing his hands together when Karen came back into the kitchen. She took one look at him and grinned.

"My, my, an honest-to-goodness snowman in my kitchen," she teased.

"I shook my coat off," he protested. "And knocked most of it off my boots."

"But you should see your hair," she said, stepping closer to brush away the lingering snow. "Even your eyelashes are covered."

As her fingers grazed his cheek, Grady felt his breath catch in his throat. The temptation to kiss her was so powerful it was almost impossible to resist. Her sweet, warm breath was fanning against his skin. Her lips looked warm and inviting. In fact, they promised the kind of heat that could chase away that last of his chill.

No, he told himself firmly. He couldn't do it. It would ruin everything. Certainly, it would destroy her fragile trust in him.

He forced himself to take a step back, to capture her hand in his and hold it away from his face.

"Thanks," he said a little too curtly. "I can finish up if you'll get me a towel."

There was a startled flash of hurt in her eyes before understanding dawned. Then, cheeks flaming, she nodded and quickly ran from the room. When she returned, they had both regained their composure.

Grady toweled his hair dry as Karen made hot chocolate. His gaze kept straying to her rigid spine, to the soft curve of her hips, to the bare nape of her neck. He wanted to trail his hand down her spine until she relaxed, to rest his palm against that very feminine backside. He wanted to press a kiss to her neck, feel the shudder ripple through her.

He wanted things he had no business wanting, he chided himself, turning away. Staying here might be a necessity tonight, but it was a bad idea. He'd honed his willpower over the years, resisted more than his share of temptation, but this…this was torment. Karen Hanson was the kind of woman made for loving— not just physically, though that was the strongest temptation at the moment—but through and through.

Was that how Caleb had seen her, Grady wondered, as a woman who deserved a carefree world? Was that why he had struggled so hard to keep this ranch afloat, to give her a home? It was funny how the last week or so had taught him a thing or two about Caleb Hanson, when his goal had been getting to know the man's wife. He found himself walking in the man's shoes, understanding his stubborn determination in a way he never had before, even admiring it.

"The hot chocolate's ready," Karen said, breaking into his thoughts. "You'd better get started on that popcorn, or the drinks will be cold before it's done."

"I just need a couple of minutes," Grady said. "Where's your microwave?"

She grinned at him. "I don't have one. You're going to have to pull this off the old-fashioned way."

His gaze narrowed at her amusement. "You don't think I can do it?"

"It will be interesting to see, won't it?" she challenged him.

He shook his head with exaggerated pity. "You've forgotten already about the bare-bones lifestyle my grandfather lives. I'm used to roughing it," he said as he reached for a covered pan. He set it on the stove, turned on the heat, then dumped the contents of the bag into the pan and covered it. "Piece of cake. You'll see."

Grady's gaze clashed with hers and held. She didn't seem to be impressed yet.

Her gaze never wavered. Time fell away as he listened to the beating of his heart, and watched the flicker of some unreadable emotion in her eyes.

"Smells like it's burning," she said cheerfully, breaking the mood and the eye contact after several minutes.

He tore his gaze away, saw smoke billowing from the pan, and muttered a soft curse. He grabbed the pan off the stove and dumped it into the sink. He could hear the few last kernels popping even as he scowled at the offending pot. He'd been oblivious when they started to pop, oblivious to everything but Karen.

Her low chuckle drew his gaze. He studied her for a second, and saw the twinkling satisfaction in her eyes.

"You did that on purpose, didn't you?" he accused.

"What?" she asked, all innocence.

"Distracted me."

"Did I? How?"

"You kept my attention so I wouldn't notice what was happening on the stove."

"Why would I do that?"

"To prove a point."

She grinned broadly. "Well, you have to admit, you were awfully sure of yourself."

"And you were willing to sacrifice the popcorn just to take me down a peg or two?"

"It seemed like a fair trade to me," she said without the least bit of remorse.

Grady sighed. "I really, really like popcorn when I watch a movie."

"We don't have to watch it," she said. "The power could go any minute, anyway, and the generator doesn't keep anything going except the furnace and the hot water heater."

He deliberately locked gazes with her, just as she'd done with him. "If we don't watch the movie, what did you have in mind?"

"We could go to bed," she said with a perfectly straight face.

A smile tugged at his lips. "Somehow I don't think you mean the same thing by that as I would."

Her gaze faltered then. She swallowed hard. "No, I imagine I don't."

"Then let's watch the movie. It's the safest thing that comes to mind at the moment."

They took their hot chocolate into the living room. Grady turned on the TV, popped the video into the player, then deliberately sat right smack in the middle of the sofa opposite it. Karen regarded him with narrowed eyes for a heartbeat, then sat next to him, albeit a careful few inches away. He barely hid a grin.

He pressed the start button on the remote, and Lauren's gorgeous face filled the screen. She was a beautiful woman, but she had nothing on the woman beside him, Grady reflected. As the images on the screen flickered, it wasn't the story, or even Lauren, that captured his attention. It was Karen.

She was totally absorbed in the romantic comedy, her eyes alternately shining with pleasure or misty with unshed tears. From time to time her lips curved into a smile.

When the movie ended, Grady couldn't have said what it was about, but he knew every nuance that had registered on Karen's face.

"That was wonderful," she said, her eyes sparkling.

"Yes, it was," Grady said, though he was talking about something else entirely. Watching her when her guard was down had been a revelation. The laughter had been close to the surface, completely uncensored. The flow of tears had been uninhibited.

He lifted his hand and touched her cheek, then brushed away the last traces of happy tears. She trembled, but she didn't move away.

Once again, it was up to him to stop, up to him to be rational. The tests were getting harder and harder...the results more and more uncertain.

"I still can't believe that glamorous woman on the screen is my friend," she said, her voice a shaky whisper. "She used to steal the Twinkies out of my lunchbox."

"Did she ever steal your boyfriends? That would be a far more serious crime."

"Never," she said fiercely. "Despite her reputation for having romances with her leading men, despite the two well-publicized marriages and divorces, the Lauren I knew was a shy girl. Most of the dates she had in high school were ones we set up for her. But even if she'd been some junior femme fatale, she would never have stolen our boyfriends. It would have gone against everything she believed about friendship.''

She looked at him. "What about you? Were you a love-'em-and-leave-'em kind of guy?''

"Nope," he said, responding to the question as solemnly as she'd asked it. "Only one girl ever stole my heart, and then she broke it. I haven't been anxious to repeat the experience. Haven't had time, either, for that matter.''

"You seem to have a lot of time on your hands now,'' she pointed out lightly. "Or do you justify all your time here as work? Part of your self-declared mission in life?''

He bit back his irritation that they were once again on the subject of her distrust of him and his motives.

"I'm here because I want to be,'' he said, choosing his words carefully. "You need some help, and I can provide it.''

"And?'' she prodded.

"That's it,'' he insisted, getting to his feet and heading upstairs before he did something to prove just how badly he wanted to stick around.

"Grady?''

He stilled, commanding himself not to turn back, fearful of what might happen if he did.

"There are towels in the bathroom, the blue ones,'' she said. "And your room's at the top of the stairs on the left.''

"And yours?'' he asked, unable to stop the question.

"Down the hall," she said

"I'll keep that in mind," he said quietly.

And in the meantime, he'd say a little prayer that it was a very long hall.

Chapter Six

Karen snapped awake in the morning to the scent of coffee brewing.

Caleb, she thought for a heartbeat, before she remembered and her mood shattered.

No, not her husband, but his worst enemy, she realized, sinking back against the pillows and drawing the covers up. The gesture was partly because it was cold, but also a halfhearted attempt to hide, to pretend that just outside her door nothing was different. Burrowing under the covers had been her way of trying to escape notice since childhood, when she hadn't wanted to leave the warmth and safety of home to go to school.

Of course, that had all changed once she had had the Calamity Janes in her life. From then on there had been no hiding. She had been anxious to get to school each morning to see what adventure Cassie had dreamed up overnight, or what treat Gina had baked in her ongoing experiments with recipes.

But that was then. Things were a whole lot more complicated in her life now. She had plenty of reasons to hide, and the most disturbing one was currently in her kitchen.

She snuggled under the quilt her mother had made for her as a wedding present and tried to imagine what it must be like outside this morning. The sun was already up, its brilliance pouring through the windows, casting fingers of warmth and light across the room. The wind had died down. In fact, it was perfectly still, as if the snow were absorbing sound.

When the scent of coffee was joined by that of bacon sizzling, Karen could no longer resist. She couldn't think of the last time someone had had breakfast on the table for her. That had always been her task, while Caleb was out tending to the animals. This time of year she had made oatmeal with raisins and warm milk to go along with the eggs and bacon Caleb had insisted on.

She pulled on thermal underwear and jeans, then deliberately chose another of Caleb's flannel shirts.

After she'd brushed her teeth, washed her face and combed her hair, she caught sight of a seldom-used bottle of perfume on the counter. What harm could there be in a little spritz? It wasn't vanity, she assured herself. Or an attempt to be alluring for Grady. It was just a little scent of lilacs to remind her of spring.

She added heavy socks, then did a haphazard job of making her bed before bracing herself and heading downstairs to find her boots...and whatever else awaited.

As she approached the kitchen, she felt amazingly

ill at ease, as uncertain as if the night had been far
more intimate and this was the uncomfortable morning after. In some ways it was worse, because the
desire had been there, shimmering between them, but
they had carefully ignored it.

Hovering just outside the kitchen door, her boots
in hand, she watched Grady at work at the stove, his
movements efficient and confident. It was a revelation
to her after a father and a husband who'd never shared
in household chores. Seeing Grady deftly flip a pan-
cake only added to his masculinity. It certainly didn't
diminish it as her father and Caleb believed it might
if they lowered themselves to help in the kitchen.

"You might as well come on in," Grady said without turning around, amusement threading through his
voice.

"Do you have eyes in the back of your head?" she
grumbled, stepping into the kitchen, dropping her
boots onto the floor and reaching for a mug. "I know
you didn't hear me. The floor didn't creak once."

"Nope. I smelled the scent of lilacs. Given the time
of year and the weather, it had to be you."

He turned, coffeepot in hand, to fill her cup. His
warm gaze rested on her in a way that left her feeling
oddly breathless. He was so at home in her kitchen,
so at ease, for an instant she almost felt as if this were
his house and she was the guest.

"Did you sleep well?" he asked.

Karen smiled at the question.

"You find that amusing?"

She nodded. "I was just thinking that you look as
if you've made yourself at home. Now you're inquiring about my night as a good host would."

He grinned. "I notice you're not inquiring about

mine, so I'll tell you. I slept very well. Had some fascinating dreams, too.''

Her breath snagged. ''Oh?''

''Shall I tell you about them?'' he inquired, a wicked twinkle in his eyes.

''Why don't we leave them to my imagination,'' she said.

He shrugged. ''It's up to you, but they certainly kept me warm.''

''Grady!''

He chuckled. ''Okay, I won't tease. How many pancakes can you eat?''

She eyed the size of them. They were twice as big around as the ones she made. ''Two,'' she decided.

''Bacon?''

She glanced at the plate and saw that he'd fried half a dozen strips. ''Two strips.''

He studied her. ''Two eggs also?''

''Nope. Only one.''

''Good. I was worried you were getting into a rut.''

''I probably am,'' she admitted, thinking about the sameness of her life the last ten years. ''But food's the least of it.''

Grady fixed his own plate and sat down opposite her. ''Can I ask you a question?''

She feigned shock. ''You're asking permission? It must be a doozy.''

''It is personal,'' he conceded. ''And you may not want to talk about it, not to me, anyway.''

Now he'd stirred her curiosity. ''Ask,'' she said.

''Do you regret marrying Caleb?'' When she started to react with indignation, he held up his hand. ''No, wait. I don't mean Caleb specifically, I guess. I know you loved him. I mean do you regret sacrificing all those things you'd hoped to do by marrying a rancher?''

There was less to offend in the way he'd rephrased the question. She took a sip of her coffee and considered it thoughtfully.

''You're right. I did give up a lot,'' she conceded eventually. ''I had so many ambitious dreams.''

''About traveling?''

''Travel, adventure, education. Not education as in school, but the kind of learning that comes with seeing places and meeting people. I wanted to feel history by standing in the middle of Westminster Abbey or Trafalgar Square, or standing on the steps of Parliament in London. I wanted to visit the Colosseum and the Vatican. I wanted to learn about artists like van Gogh and Monet and Rembrandt by standing in front of their works in the Louvre and other famous museums.''

''Yet you gave all of that up to marry Caleb,'' he said.

She met his gaze. ''Yes. Because, in the end, he mattered more,'' she said simply. ''The rest...we would have done it one day, together if...'' She sighed, battled against the familiar threat of tears, steadied her voice. ''If things had been different.''

''You never resented him?''

''Not once,'' she said honestly. ''And don't forget, I knew what I was getting into. I was raised on a ranch. This life wasn't new to me, and it has its good points.'' She glanced toward the window where tree branches were covered with blankets of sparkling snow. ''Mornings like this are among them.''

''They are, aren't they?'' he said quietly, following her gaze to the pristine white scene outside.

When he turned back to her, there was a twinkle back in his eyes. "Do you know what I like about a day like today?"

"What?"

"It gives you permission to play hooky. The roads will be impassable for hours yet. Once you've checked to make sure the horses have fresh water and feed, the day is yours."

She grinned at the boyish enthusiasm on his face and in his voice. "So, what do you do when you play hooky?"

"Well, now, that depends. When I'm all alone, I build a roaring fire, pick a book I haven't had time to read and settle down in a comfortable chair." His gaze sought hers and turned warm. "When I have a lovely companion trapped inside with me, there are all sorts of interesting possibilities."

Heat shot through her. Anticipation made her feel all quivery inside. She swallowed hard. "Such as?"

"Now don't go getting ideas," he teased. "I'm not easy. I won't be taken advantage of, just because we're locked away here all alone."

She chuckled and the tension was broken. "You're outrageous, you know that, don't you?"

"I do try. Now, seriously, what are our options? Scrabble? Cards?"

"I have a shelf filled with good books," she offered.

"Oh, no, that would be fine if we didn't have each other. Since we do, we need something we can do together." His gaze locked on hers. "Now, there you go again, getting ideas."

"I am not," she insisted, but she could feel a blush creeping up her cheeks. How could he joke so easily about an attraction that she was desperate to ignore? Perhaps because he'd had more practice at casual flirtations, while she'd had none.

"Okay, then, how about..." He paused, then said, "A jigsaw puzzle?"

She stared at him, astounded. How could he have known that she had a dozen of them stacked in a cupboard for days just like this one? Had he guessed? Or had he been snooping? Surely she hadn't mentioned it.

"Does that appeal to you at all?" he asked, his expression totally innocent. "Do you have any around?"

"Quite a few," she admitted. "But are you sure you want to do that? It seems, I don't know...a little tame, maybe?" Caleb had certainly never been interested in doing one with her. He'd considered it a waste of time to put something together, only to take it apart again. He was too practical for that.

Grady winked. "You've never done a puzzle with me. How about this? I'll go check on the horses. You clear things up in here and get us set up with the most complicated, challenging puzzle you have. I'll bring in some more wood for the fire when I come back."

She nodded. "Sounds like a plan," she agreed, already anticipating the lazy morning ahead. Even the company was surprisingly appealing. Grady continued to startle her with his unexpected insight into her personality and what would make her happy. Was that because he was incredibly sensitive and intuitive, or because he was devious and clever? For the next few hours, maybe it didn't even matter.

An hour later they were in front of a blazing fire. The damp wood was popping and snapping as it caught. Karen had chosen two puzzles, one a detailed country scene with only five hundred pieces, the other a wickedly difficult thousand-piece image of hundreds of tropical fish. She left it to Grady to decide.

"The fish," he said at once. He brought paper and pen to the table.

"What are those for?"

"To keep score, of course."

"You keep score when you put a puzzle together?"

"I told you it was more of a challenge when I did it. Are you game?"

Her competitive spirit kicked in. "Absolutely." She'd put this puzzle together once before. She knew exactly where some of the trickiest sections were and what to watch for. "How are you scoring? Total number of pieces we each put together?"

"Exactly. We have one hour."

She looked up from her assessment of the pieces spread across the table. "An hour?"

He grinned. "After that, if it's necessary, we work together to finish it. Agreed?"

"Agreed," she said, and solemnly held out her hand.

Grady's clasp was warm and brief—his attention was already totally focused on the puzzle. Before she'd even had a chance to catch her breath, he'd snapped his first two pieces together.

Karen forced her concentration back to the puzzle. She found two linking pieces of her own, then a third. Within a few minutes she had the bottom right corner of the puzzle coming together nicely.

She glanced across the table and saw that Grady was at work on the top left section, his brow furrowed, his gaze intent. His total absorption was en-

dearing somehow. It made her wonder if he would be
that totally absorbed when he was making love.

As soon as the thought crossed her mind, her
cheeks burned. No more of that, she chided herself,
forcing her gaze back to the puzzle. It would play
havoc with her concentration.

As it turned out, it already had. Though she tried
to get back into it, all the pieces began to look the
same. She tried to fit together several that were wildly
mismatched...as she and Grady were, she reminded
herself.

Stop that! she ordered herself as his knee bumped
up against hers, sending an electric current racing
down her leg. Her thoughts turned chaotic again. Suspicious, she stared at him. Had the grazing of his knee
been intentional? Was he deliberately trying to distract her? Was this payback for her game to ruin his
popcorn the night before? If so, she couldn't tell it
from his expression. He appeared completely focused,
completely oblivious to her presence, and his section
of the puzzle was growing by leaps and bounds.

She shifted her foot under the table until it found
his leg. To justify her uncharacteristic actions, she
told herself this was war as she began a slow, upward
slide, her gaze locked intently on the table as if she
had no idea what was happening beneath it. Grady
jolted as if she'd prodded him with a hot poker from
the fireplace. She bit back a grin, delighted that she
had his full attention.

That bit of distraction allowed her to quickly as-
semble several more puzzle pieces, and she grinned
as she saw she had completed the full outline of the
right side.

The next time Grady reached for a piece, she made

sure she reached for it at the same time, her hand covering his.

"Oh, sorry," she said sweetly, as she withdrew.

He watched her, his gaze narrowed. "What are you up to, Karen?"

"Up to?" she said innocently. "I just thought that piece was the one I needed."

"Did you now?" he asked suspiciously. "Where did you think it went? Show me."

She took it and tried it in the bottom corner. Of course, it didn't fit. "Guess not," she said with a shrug. She handed it back to him.

"You're dangerous," he said huskily. "You know that, don't you, Karen?"

No man had ever suggested she was dangerous, and Karen discovered she liked it that Grady had. "Remember that," she advised as she went back to work on the puzzle, deliberately ignoring him.

Naturally Grady wasn't satisfied to leave it at that. Feeling his gaze on her, she glanced up to find his dark eyes studying her intently.

"Shouldn't you be concentrating on the puzzle?" she inquired.

"You're more fascinating," he said.

Truthfully, *he* was more intriguing than the puzzle, too, but Karen didn't dare mention that. The teasing actions she had meant to distract him had affected her as well. The deliberate flirting had made her a little too aware of him as a flesh-and-blood man, instead of an abstract enemy. She was losing her grip on that negative image of him, letting the barriers crumble.

When she realized that he was no longer staring at her but at the puzzle, that he'd used these few minutes to complete another big chunk, she recognized that letting her guard down, even for a second, was a mistake. It was a lesson she needed to keep in mind.

Glancing at the clock, she saw that there were fifteen minutes left in their competition. Grady had a serious lead. She couldn't let him win. Not at this. Not at any of his games. The stakes were too high and, for one terrifying minute, she had lost sight of that.

It wouldn't happen again, Karen vowed, as she went back to work on the puzzle with total concentration. This might be just a silly contest, but Grady was clearly playing as he did everything, with a winner-take-all attitude. It would be wise to remember that, because the next time she might lose more than a game.

Grady had never expected to get turned on by doing a jigsaw puzzle. Oh, he'd always found competition to be invigorating, but arousing? Never. Which meant this had to do with his opponent.

He glanced at Karen, amused by her flushed cheeks, by the tip of her tongue caught between her teeth, as she focused totally on the puzzle. She was a feisty, sneaky competitor, far more devious than he'd ever envisioned. She had taken him totally by surprise when she'd flirted outrageously in a very successful attempt to distract him.

Not only was he distracted from the game, he was totally absorbed by the female puzzle sitting opposite him. He realized that he was no closer to his goal of understanding Karen than he had been on the day he'd decided to start spending time with her. There were too many layers, too many contradictions.

Her blind loyalty to her husband's memory bumped

up against her sense of fair play. Her wistful dreams clashed with the harsh reality of her life. She was stubborn and hardheaded, yet vulnerable. Her eyes could flash with defiance and anger one minute, with heat and desire the next. And heat and desire were what she aroused in him, on a more continual basis.

Something was happening between the two of them, but Grady was at a loss to understand it or to predict where it might lead. Nor did he dare jump to any conclusions, because one misstep could ruin everything.

The ringing of a phone jarred the peaceful ambiance. Karen looked up, startled, and maybe even a little bit afraid. Or was it guilt that caused the color in her cheeks to heighten again? Guilt that she was sharing the day with him?

It took her a minute to react, but then she bolted for the kitchen. He heard her answer the phone with a terse greeting, then her voice dropped and he could hear nothing at all.

Knowing it would infuriate her, he used the time to add another dozen pieces to his section of the puzzle. He studied her work and his own and concluded that he had the game easily won.

When she came back into the room, she looked shaken.

"Everything okay?" he asked.

She nodded, but her expression remained troubled and she stood several feet from the table, as if she didn't dare sit down and join him.

"I don't believe you," he said bluntly. "Who was on the phone?"

"Just Gina, making sure that everything was okay out here."

So far, he didn't see the problem. "And?"

Worried blue eyes finally met his. "She'd heard you were here."

"How would she hear a thing like that?" he asked.

"One of the neighbors apparently saw you turning in here earlier in the day yesterday. Somebody asked Hank about it, and he told 'em to mind their own business. Dooley apparently wasn't so circumspect."

Grady was indignant. "Seems like a lot of commotion over you having a visitor."

"Not just any visitor," she reminded him. *"You."*

"So what?"

"Grady, don't play dumb. You know how the Hansons will feel when they hear about this. It's bad enough that people are probably calling every ten seconds to report that you've been stopping by to help out. When they hear you were here overnight, they're going to go ballistic."

He reached for her hand, but she snatched it away. "Karen, nothing happened last night."

She scowled at him. "Don't you think *I* know that? But it's appearances that matter."

"Really?"

"With Caleb's parents, it is."

"And their opinion matters to you?"

"Of course it does. He was their son. This was their home. I have a duty..."

He found himself battling exasperation. "The only duty you have is to yourself."

She shook her head. "You're wrong. People don't live just for themselves. You have to consider the impact your actions could have on everyone you care about." Her gaze challenged him. "Isn't that what you're doing?"

He regarded her with confusion. "I don't know what you mean."

"Don't you? You told me you want to buy this ranch because of your grandfather," she reminded him. "It's never been about you, has it? It's been about your sense of duty toward a man you admire and love and to those who came before him, people you never knew at all."

The accuracy of her assessment made him pause. "Okay, you're right."

"So you have your obligations and I have mine. I don't want to hurt the Hansons, Grady. I really don't."

"And my being here will hurt them."

She nodded.

Because he hated seeing her so unhappy, he stood up. "I'm sure the highway has been plowed by now. My truck will make it down your driveway. I'll go." His gaze locked with hers. "If that's what you want."

"I do," she said, but there was little conviction in her voice. Clearly she was struggling with herself.

Again Grady took pity on her. He would go, but not before he stepped closer, trailed a finger along her cheek. Unable to resist, he rubbed the pad of his thumb across her lower lip, needing to know if it was a soft as it looked. It was, and it quivered beneath his touch.

"It's okay, Karen," he told her quietly.

"It's not," she said. "I shouldn't be insisting that you go. If something happens—"

"Nothing is going to happen. I'll call you when I get to my place, if it'll make you feel any better." He forced a grin. "Though I'd think you might actually feel better if I slid into a ditch."

She stared at him, clearly aghast at the suggestion. "How can you say a thing like that?"

"I am a thorn in your side, aren't I?"

"True," she admitted with her unfailing candor. Then she sighed. "But I'm starting to get used to it."

Another tiny triumph, Grady concluded. He would savor that on the long, cold, risky ride home.

Chapter Seven

Grady stayed away for two weeks. Even though it was something she'd once hoped for, Karen found herself watching the driveway day after day, regretting the attack of conscience that had had her sending him off after the snowstorm.

She knew he'd gotten home safely, not because *he'd* called, but because his housekeeper had. It was as if he'd taken her cue and decided to go one step further, cutting off all contact. The disappointment she had felt the second he had left had only grown in the days since that afternoon.

"You certainly look miserable," Gina declared when Karen drove into Winding River to have a spaghetti dinner at the restaurant where her friend was filling in as cook. Tony had used Gina's willingness to step in for him as the perfect excuse to take his wife on a long-promised trip to Italy.

"Just what every woman wants to hear," Karen said. "Maybe I should have stayed home. I can probably boil pasta as well as you can."

"Ouch," Gina protested.

"Well, I can."

"But your pasta isn't homemade. Mine is."

"You've got me there, though I doubt I'd notice the difference."

"Which brings us back to miserable," Gina said, sitting down opposite her. "I've got some time to talk. We're not that busy. What's going on?"

"Nothing," Karen said honestly. There was nothing good or bad going on in her life. Every day it was just more of the same exhausting work and loneliness. She'd had a brief respite, thanks to Grady…which made it seem even more depressing now.

"Hey, this is *me* you're talking to, not those nosy in-laws of yours," Gina said. "Tell the truth. Is this about Grady Blackhawk?"

Karen's gaze shot up. "Why would you think that?"

"Just hazarding a guess. You two were spending a lot of time together until I told you I'd heard rumors floating around town about him being at the ranch the night of the snowstorm. Is he still coming by?"

"No."

"Did you two have a fight?"

"Not exactly."

Gina regarded her with exasperation. "This is like trying to get information out of the CIA."

Karen grinned despite herself. "Sorry. I'm not being deliberately tight-lipped. I just don't know what to say. After you called, I explained what you had said, and I told him it would be best if he left. He seemed to understand.''

"But he hasn't been back," Gina concluded. "Hasn't called, either?"

"Nope."

Her gaze narrowed. "And that really bothers you, doesn't it? Were you starting to trust him, Karen? Maybe even like him? Was this turning into something for you?"

Karen felt compelled to deny it, even though the truth was that Gina had hit on the problem. "It was a pain in the neck at the outset," she said. "It's a pain in the neck now. Nothing's changed."

"Except that you've realized that the pain is actually a gorgeous, sexy man," Gina guessed, clearly not buying her disclaimer.

Karen sighed. "Yes, well, there is that."

"And that maybe you wouldn't mind getting to know him a lot better," Gina continued. "At least if there weren't all these obstacles in the way."

"But the obstacles are real," Karen said despondently. "Caleb, his parents, the ranch—how can I overlook any of that just because I've been feeling a little lonely and Grady has filled a void in my life?"

Gina stood up. "I'm getting you a glass of wine. No, a whole bottle of wine."

Karen regarded her with alarm. "I can't drink and drive all the way back to the ranch."

"You're not going to. You're going to drink and walk to my place and spend the night." Gina walked off toward the bar before Karen could protest.

While Gina was gone, the rest of her words sank in. When she returned, Karen studied her intently, then asked, "Since when do you have a place in Winding River?"

Gina winced. "You caught that, did you? Since I agreed to stick around and help Tony out. I couldn't keep crashing at my parents' place, so I rented an apartment here in town."

"For how long?"

Gina shrugged. "Yet to be determined," she said, casting a look across the dining room to a table by the window. The man who'd been hanging around off and on since the reunion was sitting there with an empty wineglass and a stack of paperwork. He looked as if he'd set up a permanent office right there. At the moment he was the only other customer.

"Do you want to tell me who he is and what's going on?" Karen asked, studying her friend's face with concern.

"Nope," Gina said.

Alarm rose as another thought occurred to her. "He's not stalking you, is he?"

"Not the way you mean," Gina said wryly. "Drink your wine. I'm going to fix your dinner. Forget spaghetti. This will make your mouth water. It will transport you straight to a trattoria in Rome."

Karen noticed that, on her way across the room, Gina paused to splash a little wine into the man's glass, though she carefully avoided his gaze, ignored whatever he said and kept right on going toward the kitchen, where the waitress was no doubt filing her nails.

Interesting, Karen thought. And troubling. Gina had never been known for her reticence. In fact, her bubbling enthusiasm and firsthand knowledge of Italian cuisine, combined with her innovative technique in the kitchen, had made her the perfect candidate for running a successful New York restaurant. She wasn't bubbling now, though. At least not with the mysterious stranger.

And in all these months there had been no mention of that New York bistro or who was running it in her absence. Direct questions had been ignored or evaded, which was very unlike the candid Gina of old.

Another mystery, Karen concluded with a sigh. Her life seemed filled with them lately. And Grady was the biggest one of all. Had he been insulted, even hurt, by her cavalier dismissal that day? Had he simply given up the fight? As incredible as that might be, it was a possibility.

Maybe he was simply away on a sudden trip. She knew he had a ranch, but he also had other business interests. Perhaps he'd had to go to Cheyenne or Denver or who knew where else he might have his finger in some corporate pie. Maybe this disappearing act had nothing to do with her at all.

She sighed at the thought. More troubling than his disappearance was her reaction to it. She missed him, dammit. As Gina had guessed, Karen had gotten used to Grady's company, exasperating as it was at times.

"It was just a habit," she muttered. Like anything else that was bad for her, it could be broken.

"Deep thoughts?" a familiar male voice inquired behind her.

Her head snapped around, her gaze clashed with Grady's, the wine she held with suddenly trembling fingers splashed on the table.

"Where have you been?" she asked before she could bite back the words. Even she recognized they were a stark contrast to her previous greetings demanding to know why he *was* there.

"Miss me?" he asked, a devilish twinkle in his eyes.

"No more than I would a swarm of bees," she retorted.

He slid into the seat opposite her, taking note of the second glass of wine. "Where's your date?"

"I'm here alone."

"Good. Then I'll join you," he said, taking a sip from the untouched extra glass Gina had left for herself.

Karen frowned, annoyed by his presumption and by her own eagerness to have him stay. "Grady, you can't just waltz in here and invite yourself to have dinner with me."

"Why not?"

"Just because."

"Because it's going to stir up more talk?" he asked, regarding her with a pointed look.

"That, too," she agreed.

"And what else?"

"Maybe I don't want to have dinner with you."

"Maybe?" he teased. "Let me know when you decide, then we'll discuss it. Until then, I'll just sit here and enjoy the wine and the vision of a beautiful woman sitting across the table from me."

"I don't want you here," she said with more conviction. "And you know perfectly well why it's a bad idea."

He studied her thoughtfully, then shook his head. "Yes, you do want me here. You just feel compelled to deny it. You're tough enough to stand up to a little idle gossip."

"If you believe that, then why did you leave the house when I asked you to?"

"Because my being there had clearly upset you and because I was way too tempted to kiss you senseless to make you forget that inconvenient conscience of yours."

"And now?"

"You're here. I happened by. I consider that fate." He smiled, then turned his attention to the menu. "What are you having?"

Because she knew from experience there was little point in arguing, she gave up. Besides, the truth was, she was so happy to see him, so happy to know that he wasn't furious with her, that her heart felt lighter than it had in days.

"I have no idea what I'm going to eat."

"You haven't ordered?"

"Gina wouldn't let me. She's fixing what suits her."

Grady nodded. "Maybe I'd better stick my head in the kitchen and make sure she fixes enough for two."

As he crossed the restaurant, Karen watched him intently. Her pulse had kicked into high gear the second she heard his voice and hadn't let up since. This wasn't good, she thought. Not good at all.

Gina came stalking out of the kitchen on Grady's heels and followed him straight to the table. Her indignant gaze came to rest on Karen. "Are you okay with this?"

"He's not going away," Karen said with an air of resignation. "I guess I'll have to make the best of it."

"I can kick him out," Gina offered.

"You and who else?" Grady demanded, regarding Gina with amusement.

Gina's gaze strayed to her mysterious man. "I can muster up some help if I need it," she declared.

"No need," Karen said. "Grady will be on his good behavior." She looked at him. "Won't you?"

He winked. "The best. And I'm a really big tipper."

Gina grinned then, apparently satisfied that there would be no fireworks. "I'm counting on it."

After she'd gone, Grady looked at Karen. "She's very protective of you."

"As you've figured out by now, I'm sure, there are five of us who grew up together. We've been best friends ever since. There's nothing we wouldn't do if one of us needed something."

"And these are the friends who are willing to bankroll your vacation?"

"Some of them, yes."

"It must be nice to have a circle of friends you can count on."

Her gaze narrowed at that. "Don't you?"

"I have acquaintances," he said with no trace of self-pity. "And I have my grandfather. That's always been enough."

She thought she detected a rare note of wistfulness in his voice. "It has been? Not now?"

His gaze met hers. "No," he said quietly. "Not now."

Deep inside, she felt something give way. It was the last of her defenses crumbling…and for the life of her, she couldn't seem to regret it.

Even though she'd been anticipating—no, dreading—the call, hearing Anna Hanson's voice on the phone first thing the next morning would have been disconcerting enough for Karen under any conditions. But Grady had arrived not five minutes earlier. He was standing right next to her. That was enough to fill her with guilt. Added to the discovery she'd made the night before about just how vulnerable she was to this man and the guilt tripled.

"Anna," she said with forced enthusiasm. "How good to hear your voice."

"Is it?" Anna said in that dire tone that meant she had plenty to say to Karen, none of it good.

Anna Hanson hadn't entirely approved of her son's choice of a wife for reasons that had never been clear. Maybe she would have resented any woman chosen by her only son.

And when Caleb had died, Anna had all but said she believed Karen was responsible in some way. Had she known that Karen, in fact, blamed herself, she would have thrown it in her face at every opportunity. Even as it was, the tension between them had been thick ever since the funeral. Anna called only when she felt duty-bound to check in on the condition of the ranch, and seemed to have no concern about how Karen was managing with her grief.

"Of course it's good to hear from you," Karen said, scowling at Grady, who rolled his eyes, clearly aware of the reason for this call. "How's everything in Arizona? Is Carl doing okay?"

"He'd be much better if we hadn't been hearing certain things," Anna said, her tone grim.

Karen barely contained a sigh. At least the woman hadn't wasted any time getting to the point. "What things?"

"That you and that terrible Grady Blackhawk have been carrying on."

"Excuse me?" Karen said, though she was less stunned by the accusation than she would have been if Gina hadn't warned her that rumors were circulating about the night of the storm. She was only surprised that they'd taken so long to reach her in-laws.

"The first time I heard it, I dismissed it," Anna claimed, sounding self-righteous. "But we've had three calls this morning alone. Apparently everyone in the entire region knows that he's spending every single day at the ranch with you. That was bad enough, but then he was there overnight. Was he sleeping with you in my son's bed?"

Karen had always tried to ignore her mother-in-law's attitude for Caleb's sake. She had wanted a smooth co-existence, if a friendship was impossible. But Caleb was no longer a consideration. She no longer had to bite her tongue. Years of pent-up anger roared through her.

"How dare you," she said sharply, aware that Grady had moved closer and laid a supportive hand on her shoulder. She shuddered at the contact, especially given the context of the conversation, but she didn't move away.

"I loved your son," she told Anna emphatically. "I never gave him or you any reason to doubt that. I certainly wouldn't do anything disrespectful of his memory under his roof."

"Then why is that man there every single day? Why did he spend the night? And how could you be seen in public with him last night, flaunting your affair in front of our friends?"

Karen wasn't exactly certain how to answer that. "He stayed the night because he was stranded by the storm. And whether you want to believe me or not, there is no affair.''

"If you say so,'' Anna said skeptically. "But that doesn't explain what he's been doing there in the first place.''

"He's been helping out.''

"You surely don't need the help of the likes of Grady Blackhawk. Or are you running the ranch into the ground?'' Anna asked bitterly.

Karen restrained her temper. Another outburst would solve nothing. "Any time you and Carl would like to come back and take over running this place, you're more than welcome to. In fact, I'd be delighted to sell it back to you,'' she said to remind the woman of the fact that she and Caleb had taken out a mortgage of their own to pay his parents the money they needed to retire. It was the size of that mortgage that had kept them in debt, but Caleb had insisted it was only fair.

"Well, I never...'' Anna said. "I'm going to put Carl on. Maybe he can get through to you.''

Karen's relationship with Caleb's father had always been more cordial. He had been as hardworking as his son. In fact, if it had been up to Carl, he would have stayed on after the funeral to help out, but Anna had been insistent that they needed to get back to Arizona where she had a brisk social calendar lined up, now that she was happily ensconced in a fancy retirement village.

"Don't mind Anna,'' he said the minute he got on the line. "She just took Caleb's death real hard. She doesn't mean half of what she says.''

"But the other half, she does,'' Karen pointed out wryly. "I've never known which half to listen to.''

"Neither, would be my advice," he said. "You doing okay, Karen? Hank and Dooley giving you enough help?"

"We're managing."

"What about this Blackhawk fellow? Has he been hanging around, like Anna hears?"

Karen sighed, glancing over at the man in question. "He wants the ranch. He's made an incredible offer."

Maybe Carl would tell her to go ahead and sell. If she had his permission, maybe this wouldn't continue to eat away at her, and she could get away from the ranch and from Grady, finally escaping all the memories that haunted her here, good and bad.

"I don't want that ranch in Blackhawk hands," Carl said flatly. "If you want to get out, I can understand that. Nobody knows better than I do what a thankless task it is trying to keep a small ranch running in the black. Just promise me you'll sell to anybody but him. Why should that man be rewarded after all the sneaky, conniving things he and his family have done to us through the years?"

Karen didn't have an argument for that. Grady had been working hard to prove that she'd misjudged him, but he hadn't offered any proof at all that he hadn't been behind the sabotage of their herd. Someone had infected those animals and set fire to that pasture. If not Grady, then who? Until she knew for certain, Carl was right. She couldn't sell to Grady.

"I won't do anything at all without talking it over with you," she promised her father-in-law.

"That's good enough for me. You take care of yourself, Karen. I don't want you wearing yourself out at your age out of some misguided sense of loyalty, you hear me? If the time comes when you can't do it or even if you just decide you want a different life, then you grab your chance. I love that land, but it's just land. It's not worth dying for, the way Caleb did.''

''I love you,'' she said to him, tears stinging her eyes.

''You, too. You were a good wife to my boy and I will always be grateful to you for that.''

Karen slowly hung up the phone, not daring to look at Grady.

''The Hansons, I presume,'' he said caustically. ''Did they manage to restore your sense of purpose?''

''I'm not going to discuss them with you,'' she said, already reaching for her coat. ''I've got work to do.''

''Where are you going?'' he asked as she pushed past him.

''To the barn. Not all of us have time to fritter away.''

He stopped her in her tracks. ''Is that what you think I'm doing around here, frittering away my time?''

Her gaze clashed with his. ''Isn't it? You have plenty of people working for you, I'm sure, people who do whatever needs doing on your ranch. I don't. If something needs to be done around here, I do it myself.''

She jerked away from his grasp and ran outside, tears streaking down her face, all but turning to ice in the frigid February air. She headed straight for the barn and Ginger's stall, leaning against the horse for comfort, absorbing her body heat.

When her tears had dried and her nerves settled, she reached for a brush and began grooming the horse as a reward for her patience. The steady strokes were soothing to both of them. Eventually she was calm enough to think about what had just happened, not just on her phone, but in her kitchen.

She had taken Anna's attack out on Grady, no doubt about it. She'd figured he deserved it, since he was the cause of it. The plain truth was, Anna had ladled on guilt and Karen had accepted it because she was riddled with guilt already. Then she had lashed out at the cause.

She owed him an apology. She was the one who'd agreed weeks ago and again the night before to his visits. She had known there would be talk, known deep down that sooner or later it would reach Caleb's parents and that there would be a price to pay.

What was one more disagreement, one more disapproving lecture, from a woman who hadn't been any less critical when Caleb had been alive?

Finished in the barn, Karen walked slowly back to the house, where she overheard Grady on the phone.

"I want it taken care of today, do you understand me? This has dragged on long enough."

Her heart thudded wildly at the implication. Was he tired of trying to outwait her? Was he somehow going to force the issue?

She let the door slam behind her and stood in front of him, her pulse thundering. "What was that about?" she demanded. "What are you up to now?"

The dismay on his face seemed proof enough of his treachery.

"You will not get this ranch," she said, jabbing a finger in his chest. Because it felt so good, she did it again, and then again, until tears were streaming down her cheeks and she was pounding on him with her fists. "You won't, dammit! I won't let you."

Grady let her rant until she wound down. Then he gathered her close, murmuring soothing, nonsensical words. Slowly she relaxed against him. Every inch of her was suddenly awakened to the sensation of their bodies pressed together, of his arms tight around her, his breath fanning her cheek.

"It's okay, darlin'. It's okay," he reassured her. "That call wasn't about the ranch, I promise. It was about something else entirely."

She wanted to believe him, wanted to believe she had misunderstood, but how could she? She lifted her head from his chest to look into his eyes. What she saw there was even more troubling than the treachery she'd suspected. There was hunger and yearning and the kind of seething passion she'd almost forgotten existed.

His gaze locked with hers, he tenderly wiped the tears from her cheeks. His thumb caressed her mouth. The flash of heat in his eyes turned brighter. The air around them suddenly felt charged with electricity…and with anticipation.

And then, before Karen could guess his intentions, his mouth covered hers. The kiss was everything she'd ever imagined—and feared. It was devastating. It was pure temptation.

And Grady had stolen it.

If he could steal a kiss so cleverly when she'd been furious with him only moments before, would stealing the land she'd grown to despise be any challenge for him at all?

Chapter Eight

The first time Grady kissed her, Karen reacted with shock and dismay. How could she have let it happen? Why hadn't she stopped it, slapped him, done anything to show her displeasure?

A quick peck on the lips could be explained away as a hit-and-run gesture, hardly worthy of protest, but this had been more than that. It had gone on and on. There had been plenty of time for the act to register and draw an appropriate protest, rather than weak-kneed compliance.

The taste and feel of him was still on her lips as she took a step back and then another, trembling with what should have been outrage but wasn't.

"Why did you do that?" she demanded, her back braced against the sink as she finally—belatedly—put as much distance as possible between them.

"Because I've been wanting to forever," he said,

not looking the least bit remorseful. In fact, he looked suspiciously as if he might intend to do it again.

And, God help her, Karen wanted him to. Her pulse was thundering like a summer storm. Her breasts ached. Any second the temptation to reach for him, to slip back into his embrace, would be too much for her.

There was no time to recite all the reasons why it was a terrible idea. Instead, she counted slowly to ten and back again, as if that alone would cool her yearning, as the same technique was used to temper anger.

She heard Grady's low chuckle and her gaze snapped to his to find amusement lurking in his eyes. "What?" she demanded.

"It's not going to work," he told her, clearly understanding the mental war she was waging. "I'm not going away and I *am* going to kiss you again. There's your fair warning. Never let it be said you didn't get one."

She swallowed hard, accepting the warning as pure truth. All that remained was the anticipation.

"When?" she asked, hoping that knowing that much would give her time to prepare, time to win the struggle with a desire that had caught her by surprise.

He tilted his head, studied her intently, then responded solemnly, "Now, I think. Before you work yourself into a frenzy worrying about it."

She gulped even as he claimed her mouth yet again with even more ingenuity, more wickedly clever passion. This time Karen wasn't simply an innocent bystander to the kiss, either. She kissed him back, responding to every persuasive nuance. All those protests and denials had been for nothing, because there was no mistaking that she was as caught up in the moment as he was.

Her head was spinning, her pulse racing. There was so much heat—too much. And the neediness, the overwhelming sense of urgency slammed through her with unexpected force, leaving her reeling. She had never expected to feel like this again, certainly never with Grady Blackhawk.

His name, his identity, finally snagged her attention, cutting through all the other commanding sensations. She was appalled and shaken that she was willingly in the arms of the enemy, though it was getting harder and harder to think of him that way.

Even so, it took her a long time to disengage from his embrace, longer still to take a faltering step back.

"This is my proof," she murmured, still dazed from the feel of his mouth on hers, but determined to inject a haughty note of disdain into her voice.

"Proof of what?" he said as he trailed more kisses down the side of her neck.

"That you're a scoundrel and a thief. You stole that kiss," she accused, managing to get the words out with a straight face, even though she knew it was a blatant lie. He had stolen nothing. She had given it to him willingly.

Laughter filled the air. Evidently he was no more convinced of the lie than she was.

"Maybe the first one, darlin'," he conceded. "But the second one you gave me of your own free will. You can't count that one against me, and I'd say it negates the implications of the first one. Once two people start to tango, so to speak, the blame pretty much falls by the wayside."

She frowned at him. "You would say that, wouldn't you? It serves your purpose."

"And what is my purpose?" he asked, studying her with mild curiosity.

"To get my land," she said at once, but she was no longer as certain as she had once been. A part of her was beginning to believe that he just might be after her, instead.

Grady went home that night and called his private detective, the one he'd had working for weeks to find out who might be behind the sabotage intended to take out the Hanson herd. Karen had walked in on him when he'd called Jarrod Wilcox earlier from her kitchen. He wanted to reemphasize to the man the urgency of the investigation. He needed results fast. He was growing less and less certain about why, though.

At first, he'd merely wanted Karen to know the truth so she could begin to trust him. He'd hoped that that would be the first step to getting her to sell the ranch to him. Now it was all tangled up in something personal. He wanted her trust, because he couldn't bear to see that condemning look in her eyes one more time.

"I told you this afternoon that this is all but impossible," Jarrod told him. "For one thing, the incidents took place a year ago or more. If there was any kind of physical evidence, it's long gone. Seems to me like you're throwing good money after bad by keeping me on your payroll."

"If that's your attitude, maybe I am," Grady snapped. "Maybe somebody else would approach this with a more positive attitude, maybe be a little more aggressive.''

''Anybody legitimate would tell you what I'm telling you—forget about this.''

''What about the mortgage? Surely there's paperwork about any attempt to buy up the Hanson note. The president of the bank didn't just make that up. He either had a letter or a face-to-face meeting.''

''He claims the latter, and he claims it was with you,'' Jarrod said.

''Since I've never set foot in that bank, he's lying, then. Who's paying him to lie?''

''Have you considered asking him that yourself? It'll be a whole lot harder for him to pull off the lie if you're looking him in the eye.''

Grady sighed. ''You have a point. I'll get on that first thing in the morning. Meantime, I want you to look into every person who owns land adjacent to the Hanson ranch. Either somebody wants that land for themselves or they have a reason for keeping me from having it.''

''Will do.''

''By the end of the week,'' Grady added.

''It's Wednesday now.''

''Then you'll just have to get your butt in gear, won't you?''

Jarrod sighed. ''I'll be in touch.''

Grady impatiently jammed the phone back in its cradle, only to realize that his grandfather was standing in the doorway, regarding him with curiosity. He crossed the room in three quick strides to embrace the man who meant more to him than anyone.

Even at seventy-five his grandfather was an impressive man. His thick black hair fell past his shoulders in braids that were streaked with gray. His tanned face was carved with deep lines, his black eyes intense, his bearing proud.

Thomas Blackhawk took a step back, his hands on Grady's shoulders, and studied his face. "You look troubled."

"Exasperated," Grady said.

"Perhaps you should spend some time with me up in the mountains," Thomas suggested. "It might give you some peace and some perspective."

"I imagine it would," Grady agreed. "But right now I don't have the time."

His grandfather's weathered face creased with a half smile. "All the more reason to come, don't you think?"

"I'll think about it," Grady promised. He gestured to a chair. "Can I get you something? Coffee? A drink? I have some of that disgusting orange soda you love so much."

"That would be good. And a man who lives on caffeine has no room to criticize my choice of beverage."

Grady brought his grandfather the bottle of soda. "What brings you all the way down here? Usually if I want to see you this time of year, I have to come to you."

"I have heard some troubling things."

Grady's gaze narrowed. "About?"

"You."

Uh-oh, Grady thought. The meddling Hansons were innocent babes in the wood compared to his grandfather. "Oh?" he said, keeping his expression neutral.

"You have been spending time with the Hanson widow, true?"

"Yes."

"Why? You are not pressuring her to sell you the land, are you?"

"We've discussed it," he said, choosing his words carefully. They had been over this ground before. But Grady believed that despite his grandfather's denials in recent years, he wanted that land returned to the Blackhawk family. He'd just tired of the futile battle.

His grandfather regarded him with resignation. "Why can't I make you see that this is unnecessary? For years I told your father to let it be, but he refused to listen. You are the same. That land means nothing to me."

"It is Blackhawk land," Grady said fiercely.

"It *was* Blackhawk land."

"It was stolen from our ancestors."

"At a troubling time in our history," his grandfather agreed. He peered at Grady intently. "Tell me something. Do you need this land for your ranch?"

"No, of course not. It's not even near here."

"Nor do I," his grandfather said. "So why are you stirring things up, if it is no longer of any importance to us?"

"It's a matter of principle," Grady said.

"Is this principle more important than the woman?"

So, Grady thought with a sigh, his grandfather had heard that there was more between Grady and Karen than a battle over acres of ranch land.

"One thing has nothing to do with the other," Grady replied, mouthing the lie that was becoming second nature to him.

"Explain that to me," his grandfather said. "It seems to me the two are inevitably intertwined."

"I can keep them separate," Grady insisted.

"Can she?" Thomas Blackhawk rose stiffly to his feet. "Think long and hard before you choose unwisely and trade one thing for another. It would not be the first time one of our people made that mistake."

"Meaning?"

"That things are not always what they seem at first glance. And there are many ways to bring things full circle."

Grady regarded him with impatience. "And I suppose that your enigmatic response is all you intend to say?"

"For now," his grandfather agreed, his eyes twinkling.

"Riddles," Grady muttered. "I ask for advice, and all I get are riddles."

"You are the brightest of my grandsons. Use your intelligence to figure them out."

"And if I can't?"

"Then listen to your heart."

His grandfather's words lingered long after he had gone. Grady was up all night thinking, but he couldn't seem to convince himself to stray from his original course of action. For too many years he had lived with the need to see that land restored to the Blackhawks. The memory of his ancestors deserved that, even if those living no longer thought it mattered.

It was only after hours of tossing and turning that he understood the second part of what his grandfather had been trying to tell him. In effect, his grandfather had given his blessing to a relationship between

Grady and Karen. But what was that nonsense about bringing things full circle?

Another riddle, he concluded with a sigh. His grandfather was a master of them. Unfortunately, Grady seldom had the patience to unravel them, not with the very real mystery of the sabotage to the Hanson herd standing between him and his goal.

Grady walked into the First National Bank of Winding River promptly at nine o'clock and headed straight for the president's office. Ignoring the secretary's indignant protests, he strolled into Nathaniel Grogan's office.

"Shall I call security, sir?" Miss Ames asked, casting a look of alarm in Grady's direction.

Grogan waved her off. "I can handle the gentleman."

"Could be you're being overly optimistic," Grady observed when the door had closed behind the indignant secretary.

"What's on your mind, Grady?"

Grady nodded at the acknowledgment of his identity. He'd known Nate for years, so it seemed highly unlikely that the man would have mistaken an impostor for him, which meant that face-to-face meeting he'd claimed had been a blatant lie.

"I'm sure you can figure that out," Grady told him.

"The mortgage on the Hanson land."

Grady gave him an exaggerated look of approval. "Bingo."

"What about it?"

"Apparently you told Caleb Hanson that I tried to buy up that mortgage. You told the same thing to Jarrod Wilcox. Yes or no?"

"I told them that, yes."

"Even though you know it's a blatant lie."

"I don't know that." Grogan reached into his desk drawer and pulled out a file. "Here's the paperwork, all filled out nice and proper. That's your signature at the bottom."

Grady's gaze narrowed as he studied the paper. "It's a damn fine forgery," he said at last.

"Are you telling me that's not your handwriting?" the man asked, clearly taken aback.

"That's what I'm telling you. I never filled out that paperwork. And whoever witnessed it and said I did is lying."

The old man seemed shaken by his vehemence. "Let me get Miss Ames in here. That's her notary seal on this."

He buzzed for his secretary. "In here now, Miss Ames."

The door opened at once, but the woman was slow to enter. "Yes, Mr. Grogan?"

"I want you to take a look at something."

She edged around Grady, then took the papers her boss held out.

"Is that your stamp on there?" Grogan asked.

She looked it over carefully, then nodded.

"And is this the man you saw sign those papers?" he demanded.

Another flicker of alarm flashed in her eyes as she glanced Grady's way. Her response was inaudible.

"What was that?" Grogan snapped. "Speak up, Miss Ames."

"I said no, sir. I've never met this gentleman."

"*This* is Grady Blackhawk," Nate told her. "Now my next question is, who in hell signed the papers?"

Miss Ames seemed to shrink inside her smart business suit. "I don't actually know," she said, then burst into tears.

Both men stared at her incredulously, but Grady was the first to speak. "Aren't you supposed to witness something before using your seal?"

Her head bobbed as the tears continued to fall. "Yes, but these were on my desk one morning with a note to put the seal on them and leave the file for Mr. Grogan. That's what I did. I thought it must be really urgent." She regarded her new boss with dismay. "I thought it was what you wanted, that it wouldn't matter if I broke the rules since you were the one telling me to do it."

The bank president simply stared at her. "I know you've only been here a short time, but have I ever asked you to do anything dishonest?"

"No, sir. That's why I thought it must be very important."

"And you have no idea who put the papers there?"

"None. They were there when I arrived for work. You were in your office, so I was sure you'd left them, just like the note said."

"I don't suppose you kept the note," Nate said.

She shook her head. "No, sir."

Grogan sighed heavily. "You may go, Miss Ames."

"You're…you're not firing me?"

"Not at this time," he said. "Not until we get all of this sorted out, at any rate. But if I find you know more than you've told us just now, you *will* be out of here. Am I making myself perfectly clear?"

Her head bobbed. She left the room looking so terrified that Grady almost felt sorry for her.

"I apologize," Grogan said. "I don't know what she could have been thinking."

"That she was doing you a favor, I'm sure," Grady told him wryly. "Obviously she's very loyal to you."

"Or to someone else," Grogan said wearily. "I'll straighten this out. I promise you that. And I will call Mrs. Hanson and explain things to her."

Grady nodded. "I wish you would. And one more thing. Were you the one who warned Caleb Hanson about this so-called attempt on my part to buy up his mortgage?"

"Yes. I saw to it that the application was denied and then told him what was going on. He and his family have banked here for years. I thought he had a right to know."

"Who else could have left those papers on your secretary's desk, especially before she arrived in the morning?"

"Anyone who works here. The other employees arrive here around eight. Miss Ames drops her son off at school. She doesn't arrive until closer to eight-thirty. It wouldn't take a minute to drop off the file. People leave papers on Miss Ames's desk all day long. No one would think a thing about it."

"But it couldn't have been an outsider, correct? It had to be someone working here?"

"So it seems." He looked Grady in the eye. "I'll get to the bottom of it. You have my word on that."

Grady nodded. He didn't doubt that Nathaniel Grogan's intentions were honorable, but as Jarrod Wilcox had already pointed out, this incident, like the others, had taken place long ago. Finding answers wasn't going to be simple. People's memories faded. Except, of course, for the person who'd done it. He or she wouldn't have forgotten. But could the wrongdoer be persuaded to tell the truth?

"I'll hold you to that," he said as Nate walked with him onto the main floor of the bank.

Just as they stepped into the marble-floored lobby, Karen walked through the front door, took one look at the two of them and turned pale. Then bright patches of color flared in her cheeks right before she turned and fled.

"Dammit," Grady muttered, and took off after her. He knew what she was thinking, knew she was adding up two and two and coming up with a hundred and ten or whatever number would be most damning.

He caught up with her halfway down the block and fell into step beside her. She didn't even glance over at him.

"Good morning," he said, being deliberately upbeat.

"I have nothing to say to you."

"That's fine, because I have quite a lot to say to you," he said, steering her into Stella's before she could protest. He knew her well enough to understand that she wouldn't make a scene, not here in front of her friend Cassie, who was staring at them, clearly ready to intercede.

"This looks like a nice quiet place to talk," Grady said tightly as he aimed for the booth in the back.

He stood there until she sank onto the seat with a resigned sigh, then he slid in next to her just to be sure she couldn't bolt before they had this out.

"Everything okay?" Cassie asked, her worried gaze on Karen.

"Fine," Grady said. "Bring us two cups of coffee." He glanced at Karen. "Have you had breakfast yet?"

"It's after ten. What do you think?"

He bit back a grin, then glanced up at Cassie. "I guess the coffee will do for now."

He noted that Karen's hands were folded primly on the table, that her gaze was everywhere but on him. Those angry patches of color in her cheeks hadn't faded. He warned himself to give it another couple of minutes before saying anything. Maybe once she'd had her coffee, her temper would die down and she'd be ready to listen to reason.

Cassie brought the steaming cups to the table, then lingered, but when neither Karen or Grady looked up, she sighed and walked away.

"I suppose you were wondering what I was doing with Nate Grogan," he said finally.

"I don't think it takes much imagination to figure that out," she snapped. "Did he agree to let you buy up the mortgage this time?"

"I never tried to buy the blasted mortgage," Grady retorted. "Not today. Not two years ago."

"So you say."

"Ask Grogan. He intends to call you to explain what happened anyway."

"I'm sure he'll say whatever you want him to say," she said.

"He didn't before, did he? Wasn't he the one who called Caleb to tell him what I was supposedly up to?"

She hesitated at that. "Yes," she conceded.

"Well, today he found out that I was not the person who filled out that original paperwork. I'm sure he'll tell you that if you ask."

She turned to him at last, her blue eyes filled with confusion. "But the papers…?"

"They were forged by someone and later notarized by a loyal secretary who thought she was doing what Grogan wanted her to do."

Her gaze searched his and Grady thought he saw a faint flicker of hope in her eyes. "Honestly?"

"I won't lie to you, Karen. I haven't before and I won't start now. I want that land, but I have never done anything devious or underhanded to try to get it."

A sigh seemed to shudder through her at that. "I want to believe you," she admitted.

"Then do it," he pleaded. "Believe me. Trust me."

"If only it were that simple," she whispered.

She didn't have to say what she was really thinking. Grady knew. Caleb had labeled him the enemy. How could he possibly overcome the accusations of a dead man, especially a dead man that she had loved with all her heart?

At that moment, for the first time, Grady understood the true meaning of hatred and jealousy. He hated Caleb Hanson, not for all of the lies he had believed about Grady and shared with his wife in the past, but for his ability to rob them of a future even from the grave.

Chapter Nine

Something had changed in that split second when Grady had looked into Karen's eyes at Stella's. It was as if a light had gone off inside him, as if he'd been defeated. It wasn't long before he'd made his excuses and left, leaving her staring after him in confusion.

She had told herself then that it would pass, that things would return to normal, that he would pop up when she least expected him at the ranch, but it hadn't happened that way. Just as he'd disappeared before when she'd hurt him, he hadn't been around for days now. Even Hank and Dooley, who had regarded him with suspicion from the beginning, had commented on his absence.

''Thought he was becoming a permanent fixture around here,'' Dooley said, a hint of disapproval plain in his voice.

''Well, he wasn't,'' Karen said defensively. Hiding

her confusion behind anger, she added, "And we don't have time to stand around gabbing about a man who had no business being here in the first place."

"Fine by me," Dooley said.

"And me," Hank said fervently. "The boss never did like him."

"I'm the boss now," Karen reminded him. "You need to worry about what *I* like."

Dooley's eyes widened. "Are you saying you trust a scoundrel like Grady Blackhawk?"

"He's not a scoundrel," she said. "And what I was saying is that you both have work to do. Didn't I ask you to finish checking that fence today? I saw another section down when I drove back here yesterday. We're going to be moving the herd in a few weeks and I don't want them wandering off our land. We can't afford to lose a single head."

"Yes, ma'am," Dooley said, his tone respectful, even if he was regarding her with a worried frown that suggested he wasn't entirely certain she was in command of things.

After both men had left, she sat down with a sigh. Who was she kidding? She might be in charge, but she was only holding on to this place by a thread. She knew well enough what needed to be done, but she didn't have the resources to make much of it happen. Lately it seemed she lacked the stamina as well. She simply wanted to crawl under the covers and sleep the winter away.

For a brief time Grady's presence had stirred her out of that depressing inertia, but now that he was no longer around, she couldn't seem to shake it.

The welcome ringing of the phone jarred her out of her misery.

"Hey, girl," Lauren said, her cheerful voice bringing a much needed smile to Karen's lips.

"Hey, yourself. What's up in Tinseltown? I need some hot Hollywood gossip to perk me up."

"Since when do you care about celebrity gossip?"

"It's the closest I'm likely to come to having any glamour in my life," Karen said. "Come on. Spill something absolutely titillating."

"Sorry. I've been holed up trying to learn my lines for this new movie. Brad Pitt could get married and I wouldn't know it."

"Brad Pitt *did* get married," Karen pointed out with a chuckle. "Ages ago, in fact."

"See what I mean? I'm oblivious."

"What good is it having a friend who's a superstar if you never know any hot secrets?"

"I do know one," Lauren retorted. "I know that a certain rancher has been seen hanging out with her mortal enemy. Quite an intense little tête-à-tête from what I heard."

"Cassie blabbed," Karen said with a resigned sigh. She should have known her friend would make way too much out of that public appearance she and Grady had made at Stella's. It had probably taken all of fifteen seconds for her to spread the word to the others.

"I never reveal a source," Lauren said loftily. "So, what's the scoop with the sexy Mr. Blackhawk? Are you two becoming an item after all?"

"Don't be ridiculous," Karen snapped, pushing back the thought of those two steamy kisses. "Even if I was attracted to him, which I'm not, how could I get involved with Grady?"

"Because of Caleb," Lauren said flatly.

"Of course because of Caleb."

"You have to live your life for *you* now," Lauren reminded her, her tone gentle. "I'm not saying you shouldn't remember Caleb, but you can't take on his baggage, Karen. If you like Grady, if you want to spend time with him, that's your decision to make."

"Not according to the Hansons," Karen said dryly.

"Oh, what do they know?" Lauren said, dismissing the importance of the opinion of Karen's former in-laws. "Besides, they're in Arizona."

"With a direct hotline to the gossip in Wyoming," Karen reported.

"Ignore them," Lauren advised.

"How can I? They're Caleb's parents."

"So naturally they're going to be upset if you get involved with someone new. They'll get over it."

"Not if it's Grady," Karen said flatly.

"Then you *are* interested," Lauren said, seizing on her slip and obviously concluding that Karen regretted being unable to act on her fascination with the man.

Karen sighed. "I don't know how I feel about him."

"Is he pressuring you to decide that right this second?"

"No. Actually he hasn't been around much lately. Not since the morning Cassie saw us together. I think something I said or did upset him, but I can't imagine what. He's a very complex man."

"A break may be exactly what you need. Give it some time. You're a smart woman. You'll sort out your feelings when the time is right." Lauren hesitated, then asked, "Do you want me to come home? I'm a pretty good judge of character."

"Oh, really? I can list two lousy marriages that say otherwise."

"Ouch," Lauren said. "No one can see their own mistakes until it's too late. Everyone else's, however, are crystal clear. An outside opinion wouldn't hurt and I can be there tomorrow."

"No. You've put your career on hold enough for me as it is. I can't ask you to come running every time I get scared."

"Scared?" Lauren teased. "Of Grady or yourself?"

"Maybe both," Karen admitted.

"You listen to me, Karen Hanson. Nobody I know has a better head on her shoulders than you do. Trust your instincts. And any time you want me there for backup, you call. I can drop everything and be there in a few hours. To tell the truth, I like feeling needed for a change. Say the word and I'll be back there mucking out stalls and working with the horses for as long as you need me."

Karen was so startled by the heartfelt sincerity of the offer that she was at a loss for words. It wasn't the first time the offer had been made, but something in her friend's voice suggested that she was truly hoping to be asked to rush home.

"Stunned into silence?" Lauren asked.

"Truthfully, yes. You've hinted around about wanting to come home for good, but that's the first time you've come right out and said it. What's wrong, Lauren? What haven't you been telling us?"

"There's nothing wrong," her friend assured her. "Nothing I can put my finger on anyway. I'm sure whatever it is, I'll get over it. But the offer stands, no matter what. If you need me, just say the word."

"Thank you," Karen said softly. "And...Lauren?"

"What?"

"If you need to be here, don't wait for an invitation. I've got a room waiting any time you want to come. I mean that. And if it's hard physical work you're looking for, I can supply that, too."

"I know you mean it. and I love you for saying it. Take care, sweetie."

"You, too."

Karen had barely hung up when she realized she wasn't alone. She turned to find Grady standing just outside the screen door. Still troubled by her conversation with Lauren, she barely spared him a glance. And this time, she refused to get her hopes up. His habit of coming and going when she least expected it was too disconcerting.

"Anything wrong?" he asked, his expression concerned as he stepped inside without waiting to be invited.

"Not with me," she said, injecting a false note of cheer into her voice. She was not going to discuss Lauren's odd mood with a man she didn't entirely trust. If it wound up being splashed all over the tabloids, she would never forgive herself.

Even as the thought of Grady pitching such personal information to a tabloid ran through her mind, she scolded herself over the absurdity of it. Why would he do such a thing? He certainly didn't need the money. And he was trying to prove to her that he was trustworthy. Wouldn't such a deliberate act of betrayal be counterproductive? It just proved how deep her own distrust ran.

"I thought I'd stop in and let you know that I'll be

out helping Hank and Dooley today. The fence along the highway is down.''

''I know. I spotted it yesterday. They're out there now. They can handle it.''

''I'm sure they'd be grateful for an extra pair of hands.''

Her gaze narrowed. ''Look, it's been obvious the past few days that you have a life of your own to live. You don't have to keep doing this.''

''Doing what?''

''Pitching in around here. Stay home and take care of your own chores.''

Amusement lurked in the depths of his eyes. ''So you did miss me?''

''I never said that.''

''You didn't have to.''

She frowned at him. ''Is that why you stayed away, so I'd miss you?''

''No,'' he said curtly. ''Now let me make this clear for the last time. I don't mind helping out around here. I like the company.''

She regarded him with skepticism. ''Hank and Dooley's?''

''Hardly,'' he said, grinning at last. ''But the boss lady has a certain way about her that I find intriguing.''

Her heart fluttered at the compliment. ''Is that so?''

He nodded. ''Besides that, she owes me dinner. Our deal's not over.''

''I thought you'd forgotten about that. Besides, the two weeks were up long ago.''

''We missed a few nights,'' he reminded her.

''I never gave you a rain check.''

"But you wouldn't renege on a deal, would you? Doesn't that go against that conscience of yours?"

"I suppose."

"That's settled, then. And just so you know, I have a real hankering for apple pie."

"Stella's is good," she told him.

"But I'll bet yours is better." His gaze caught hers. "Still warm from the oven with a big scoop of vanilla ice cream melting into all the little crevices."

Karen swallowed hard. Somehow he had managed to make a perfectly ordinary slice of pie sound like something wickedly sensual. Or was that just her state of mind?

"How about it?" he asked. "Pie for dessert?"

She gave him a resigned look. "I'll see what I can do."

He winked at her. "I'll be counting on it."

Don't, she thought to herself after he'd gone. *Don't count on me, Grady.*

Because the truth was, if push came to shove, she had no idea which of the men in her life she'd choose…a ghost or the flesh-and-blood man who was tempting her more and more each day, despite his entirely too unpredictable comings and goings.

Grady heard the argument long before he spotted Hank and Dooley.

"I say we've got to tell her," Hank shouted fiercely. "The woman has a right to know that someone deliberately cut this fence."

"Mrs. Hanson's got enough on her mind," Dooley argued. "We're taking care of it, aren't we? There's no harm done. Why get her all worked up about a problem that won't exist after today?"

Grady crested the hill and spotted the two hands squared off, a section of barbed wire in Hank's hands.

"I'm telling you she needs to know that somebody's out to get her," Hank countered. "She ought to be calling the sheriff. This isn't right." His gaze narrowed as he looked at Dooley. "Or is there some particular reason you don't want the sheriff involved?"

The old man drew back his fist and aimed a punch straight for Hank's face. It landed solidly, snapping the younger man's head back.

Grady leaped from the saddle and got between the two men. "Okay, enough. What the hell's gotten into you two?"

Whatever distrust they felt toward him was apparently less than they were feeling about each other at the moment, because both men started hurling accusations so fast and furiously, Grady could barely keep up.

"Hold it!" he commanded finally. "One at a time. Dooley, you first."

Hank glared at Grady as a look of satisfaction spread across the old man's face.

"Like I was trying to tell this pea-brain here, the boss already has too much on her mind," Dooley said. "There's no need to worry her with this latest incident, since we're taking care of it."

"The incident being that someone deliberately cut the barbed wire?" Grady concluded.

"Exactly," Hank said, holding out the section of wire. "Cut through, clean as a whistle. This is new fence, too. Put it in myself just last spring."

Grady didn't like the implication one bit. Once again, someone was trying to sabotage the Hanson operation. It didn't take a genius to figure out that the blame was going to fall on his shoulders sooner or later. That raised those same two interesting possibilities again. Either someone wanted to force Karen out of business for their own reasons, or they wanted to cast more doubt on his integrity simply to keep her from selling to him.

"Who owns the land on the other side of the highway?" he asked Dooley.

"Tate McDonald."

The name meant nothing to Grady. "Has he been around long?"

"Bought the place eight, maybe nine years ago," Hank said. "About the same time I came to work for the Hansons."

"Has he been looking to expand?" Grady asked.

Both men exchanged a look, then shook their heads.

"He's not here much," Dooley said. "Spends most of his time in California, from what I hear. His foreman runs the place. They keep a small herd over there, nothing like what Duke Walters had when he owned it."

That didn't mean that McDonald didn't aspire to having a much bigger operation in the future. Grady resolved to find out what he could about the man.

He already knew that the land to the west had been owned by the same family for sixty years—the Oldhams—and that the property due north belonged to Jack Fletcher, a cantankerous ex-rodeo star who trained horses and whose daughter, Maggie, had a difficult streak of her own. None of them struck him as the kind of people who'd try to force a neighbor out of business, but he'd have Jarrod Wilcox do some checking, just in case.

Grady took the piece of wire from Hank. "I'll hang on to this. For the time being, let's not say anything to Karen. Both of you keep your ears open when you go into town. See if anybody's bragging about being up to some mischief out this way. I'll check out this Tate McDonald."

Both men regarded him skeptically. "Isn't it to your advantage if somebody *is* stirring up trouble for Mrs. Hanson?" Hank asked. "If she goes under, you can buy this place for next to nothing."

"I've already made her an offer for a good deal more than the land is worth. I won't renege on that."

Dooley snorted. "Doesn't mean you wouldn't like to get it for less."

"You can believe me or not, but I'm not interested in ruining her," Grady said flatly. "She'll get a fair price if she decides to sell. And if she sells, it won't be because I've done something to make her desperate."

Dooley regarded him intently. "And you swear you're going to get to the bottom of this latest damage?" he asked.

"I swear it."

Once again, the two men exchanged a look, then seemed to reach a conclusion.

"All right, then," Dooley said. "But we're keeping an eye on you."

Grady bit back a grin at the warning. "I wouldn't have it any other way."

Karen was getting better at gauging Grady's moods. She didn't allow herself to consider what that meant. All that mattered was that he hadn't been himself since he'd returned from working on the downed fence. He was virtually silent all through dinner and as soon as he'd finished his serving of pot roast, he excused himself.

Karen scowled as he rose from his place at the table. "Okay, that's it. Sit back down, Grady Blackhawk."

Clearly startled by the command, he stared at her. "What?"

"I said to sit down." She frowned until he'd complied. "Now tell me what has you in such a foul mood."

"I'm not in a foul mood," he insisted, looking vaguely bewildered by the accusation.

"Okay, maybe that's the wrong word, but you certainly aren't yourself. You haven't been since you got back."

"I just have a few things on my mind."

"That's obvious enough. What things?"

"Nothing worth mentioning," he insisted.

"Or nothing you want to get into with me?" she challenged.

A guilty expression passed across his face. "Why would you say something like that?"

"Because you usually have plenty to say. Because you're the one who wanted to share these little getting-to-know-you meals, and you haven't said two words all evening. Because you all but begged me to bake you an apple pie, and now that I have, you're about to walk out the door without even tasting it. I'd say the evidence is overwhelming."

A grin tugged at his lips. "Is that so, Sherlock? Any other clues you'd care to mention?"

"No, I think that about does it," she said, arms folded across her chest. "I've said my piece. Now it's time for you to say yours."

"And if I don't?"

"Then you'll sit there until you think better of it."

This time he had the audacity to laugh. "Who's going to make me?"

"Me," she declared.

"Oh, really? Now that is a fascinating prospect. Care to share your tactics for keeping a man who's twice your size where you want him?"

"You don't want to know," she said. "Trust me, though. I can do it." She wasn't exactly sure how, but she would manage it, if it came to that. "Now, talk. What happened when you were with Hank and Dooley? Did the three of you get into it about something? I know they distrust you, but they're just being protective of me."

"I know that. And I respect the fact that they're loyal to you."

"Then you didn't have an argument?"

"No."

She regarded him with exasperation. "But something did happen?"

He beamed at her. "I'll take that pie now. Make it a big piece with lots of ice cream on top."

"Not a chance. It's too late for that. I want to know what went on out there today or that pie goes straight into the garbage."

Grady sighed heavily. "You're a very persistent woman, you know that?"

"Yes," she said proudly.

"It's a very annoying trait."

"I suppose that depends on your point of view," she countered.

"I imagine I could distract you, if I wanted to," he said, eyeing her thoughtfully.

"I doubt that."

"Are you challenging me to try?"

Karen spotted the spark of mischief in his eyes and realized that she'd just made a serious tactical error. Before she could correct it, he was on his feet and reaching for her.

With a look of grim determination, he slanted his mouth across hers. Whatever his intention, though, whether to silence her or challenge her, it quickly became something else entirely. The coaxing kiss turned greedy. Gentle persuasion became breath-stealing hunger.

All thoughts about winners and losers in their battle of wits fled as they set a new, common goal: passion. Karen's head went spinning, her pulse ricocheted wildly, her blood heated and pooled low in her belly.

This is wrong, she thought. *Wrong, wrong, wrong.*

And yet she couldn't seem to stop, couldn't seem to pause even long enough to catch her breath. A frantic neediness was making her breasts ache and her body eager. Grady had moved beyond kisses now. His hands were everywhere, gentle, persuasive, provocative.

Karen felt the buttons on her dress give way, felt the cool air against her overheated skin, then the warmth of Grady's clever caresses as they streaked fire in their path. She wanted things she had never expected to feel again, wanted to feel gloriously alive and loved and irresistible. Grady was giving her all of that with his wicked kisses and increasingly intimate touches.

"Not here," she pleaded, when her dress was in a tangle around her feet and her bra was across the room.

"Tell me where," he said, scooping her into his arms.

"Upstairs."

At the top of the stairs, he hesitated, and so did she. Not in her room, not in the bed she'd shared with Caleb.

"Over there," she said, gesturing toward the guest room with its colorful quilt on an antique iron bed.

There were no memories in this room, no personal mementos of her years with Caleb.

The sheets were crisp and smelled of sunshine, not the lingering—or imagined—scent of a familiar aftershave. The mattress was firm, not shaped by years of accommodating two bodies that slept curved together in the middle.

She couldn't help thinking of the contrasts as Grady lowered her onto the bed, then slid in next to her, his gaze tender as he slowly stripped away her remaining clothes. The trip to the second floor had eased the tension, the frantic need, but with one glance, one touch, he was able to bring it back until she was lying there trembling and desperate for the feel of him deep inside her.

She tugged at his shirt with impatient fingers, pushing it up and over his head, then setting to work on the snap of his jeans with total concentration. She couldn't seem to manage it, though. Her fingers trembled and, next to the heat of his bare belly, they felt icy cold. He rested his hand atop hers, then met her gaze.

"It's okay. There's no rush," he reminded her.

"There is," she insisted, struggling to free herself from his grasp so that she could finish what they had begun.

She almost missed the flash of wariness in his eyes, it came and went so quickly. But it had been there and for an instant, she felt a flicker of shame.

"I'm sorry," she whispered, her voice ragged.

"Why?"

"I don't want you to think I'm using you, that I just want this to be over with."

His smile was tinged with unmistakable sadness. "Isn't that the truth, though? At least part of it?"

"Maybe," she finally confessed in a small voice. "I want you, Grady, but I'm scared."

"Of what?"

"That it's for all the wrong reasons, just like you said."

He rolled away from her, locked his hands behind his head and stared at the ceiling until his breathing steadied. Karen felt bereft, but she didn't pursue him, didn't dare touch him the way she desperately wanted to.

Finally, when she thought she wouldn't be able to bear the tension building inside her for another second, he reached for her hand, pressed it to his lips. "Another time," he said quietly and without rancor.

Tears stinging her eyes, she reached for the sheet, clutched it to her bare breasts. "Are you sure?"

His gaze met hers. "Oh, darlin', if I am sure of anything in this world, it's that. There will be another time for this, for the two of us. And when it happens, we'll both be sure it's the right thing for the right reasons.''

A smile curved his lips. ''Now come over here and cuddle up beside me.''

Sheet firmly tucked in place, she slid closer until she could feel his heat warming her and the steady beating of his heart beneath her ear. And in that moment, her heart filled with gratitude and maybe something else, something that felt an awful lot like the first amazing moments of falling head-over-heels in love.

Chapter Ten

With Karen curved securely against him, Grady was having a hard time thinking straight, but he forced himself to concentrate on that severed barbed wire. It was about the only thing sufficiently fascinating to distract him from the warmth of her body curled next to his.

First chance he got, he was going to track down Tate McDonald and then get his private investigator doing checks on all of the neighboring property owners. One of them was holding a grudge against Karen, or against him. Since he'd never even met McDonald and barely knew the Fletchers or the Oldhams, it seemed likely the dispute was with Karen. Either way, it needed to be settled before things got ugly.

Karen sighed softly, her breath stealing across his bare chest and ruining his concentration. He thought he'd been rather clever at distracting her from all of her questions earlier, even if the outcome had been less than what he'd anticipated. He could wait until she was ready to make love, even if it was getting more and more difficult.

She moaned and snuggled more tightly against him. The sheet slipped away, revealing way too much of an alluring breast, a taut dusky nipple. His breath caught in his throat as he struggled yet again against temptation. He was more sinner than saint, and this was too much.

Gently he shook her awake, tugging the sheet back into place as her eyes blinked open, registering first surprise, then sleepy delight, then worry as she realized she had fallen asleep in his arms. The reactions pretty much summed up their relationship, a curious mix that had kept Grady off guard for weeks now. He'd tried staying away twice now, but it hadn't worked. He'd concluded he was going to have to see this through to whatever ending it was headed for.

"I must have fallen asleep," she said, gathering the sheet more securely around her. "I'm sorry."

"Don't be. There is nowhere I'd rather be."

"Really?" she asked skeptically. "You seemed to be in an awfully big hurry earlier. Don't think I've forgotten that."

He sighed. "I was hoping you had."

"Not that the distraction wasn't fascinating," she said, "but I have a very good memory."

"Apparently," he agreed, thinking of more than her interest in his earlier activities. She also had a very long memory when it came to her late husband's prejudices.

"So?" she prodded.

He regarded her with feigned innocence. "So?"

She nudged him sharply in the ribs with her elbow. "Don't play dumb, Grady. I want to know what had you so distracted over dinner. What happened when you were with Hank and Dooley? Did it have something to do with the fence?" Sudden understanding spread across her face. "Was it deliberately cut?"

The woman was too smart for her own good and Grady wasn't about to lie to her. "Yes," he said tersely.

"But who…?"

He noticed that she didn't immediately jump to the conclusion that he might be responsible. That was progress, he supposed.

"We're going to find out," he told her. "As soon as I get home, I'm going to start making calls."

"Which explains why you were so anxious to get out of here earlier," she concluded.

"Exactly."

"Make the calls from here," she said. "I want to know what you find out."

He nodded and reached for his jeans. When he was dressed, he glanced back at her tousled hair and the rumpled sheets. It looked as if much more had gone on in that bed, he thought with regret. Apparently Karen could read him even better than he'd realized. Her expression faltered.

"I'm sorry," she whispered.

He bent down and kissed her thoroughly. "You don't ever have to be sorry for not doing something you're not ready for. I can wait."

Her gaze searched his. "Can you?"

"For you? Absolutely."

She returned his gaze, her expression earnest, her

brow puckered. "I can't promise I will ever be ready."

"You will be," he said with total confidence. He believed that as he hadn't believed in anything else in a very long time.

Karen took her time before following Grady downstairs. She needed to think about what had happened...and what hadn't. She also wanted to absorb Grady's easygoing acceptance of all of it. The lack of pressure—the willing restraint—had been a surprise. She'd always believed him to be a man who simply took what he wanted. In fact, hadn't she counted on it earlier, expecting him to ride roughshod over her doubts, leaving her no choice but to make love?

But, then, there had been a lot of things she'd thought about Grady that she was discovering to be untrue. He was kind and thoughtful and unfailingly decent, at least in his treatment of her. She was beginning to doubt that he had ever been the thief and scoundrel Caleb had accused him of being.

More surprising than Grady's behavior in the past few hours was her own. She had nearly made love with a man she'd been taught to distrust. More significant, she couldn't seem to make herself regret it. In fact, if she was feeling any regrets at all, it was that she had faltered along the way and still didn't know what sort of magic she might have found in Grady's arms.

She moaned and covered her face. What was happening to her? How had she let this happen? How had she allowed it to go so far? And why didn't she feel the least bit guilty about any of it?

Because she had no answers—and was fairly certain she wouldn't like any of them, anyway—she hopped out of bed, took a quick shower, then joined Grady downstairs just as he hung up the phone. His expression was grim.

"What?" she said at once. "Have you found something?"

"Only that Tate McDonald is a very wealthy absentee owner, that your other neighbors are in debt, but no more so than any other small rancher, and that if anyone has a vested interest in ruining you, it's me." He shrugged. "That's the consensus, anyway."

"Well, we both know that's not true," she said.

He gazed into her eyes. "Do *you* know that?" he asked, his expression intent.

Karen nodded slowly, her gaze never shifting from his. "I do," she assured him, startled to find that she meant it.

Satisfaction spread slowly across his face. He touched her cheek. "Thank you."

"Don't thank me. You've more than proved yourself to me." She reached for the pot of still-warm coffee and poured two cups. "Now we just have to determine who's out to destroy me and ruin your reputation at the same time."

He grinned. "Simple as that, huh?"

"I didn't say it was going to be easy," she said, getting a notebook and pen from a drawer by the refrigerator. "We just have to be systematic and logical."

"In that case, I need that pie you promised me," Grady declared. "I can only be logical on a full stomach."

When she started to stand, he waved her back to her chair. "I can do it. Do you want some?"

"Of course."

He cut two big slices, retrieved the ice cream from the freezer and added huge dollops on the pie. She grinned at the size of the portions.

"Obviously you're planning on a long night," she commented.

"A very long night," he agreed.

One they wouldn't be spending together in bed, she thought with more than a little twinge of regret. Oh, well, the die had been cast earlier in the evening, anyway, and it was for the best. They'd both decided that. At least for now.

She took a bite of pie, savoring the burst of apple and cinnamon and sugar on her tongue, then picked up her pen. "Let's start with this McDonald person, since he's a stranger. What have you found out about him?"

"Just what I told you, that he has a lot of money and he's dabbling in ranching."

"You've never had any dealings with him?" she asked.

"None at all."

"Then we can assume for the moment that there are no grudges."

"How about you? Have you had any run-ins with him?" Grady asked.

"Never met him."

"Okay, then, how about the Fletchers? They've been the Hansons' neighbors for years. Have they always gotten along?"

"Always," Karen said, but her expression turned thoughtful. "Of course, there might have been a prob-

lem when Caleb decided to marry me. I think Maggie
Fletcher had her eye on him, and her father really
wanted the match.''

Grady nodded. ''Jealousy. That's always a good
motive for revenge, but Maggie doesn't strike me as
the type of woman to go around poisoning cattle or
cutting fences. How about you? What do you think
of her?''

Karen considered the woman who'd made no secret
of her infatuation with Caleb. Tall and slender, with
a no-nonsense manner, Maggie had always been polite, if distant, with Karen. There had never been any
question of them becoming close friends. Even if
Caleb hadn't stood squarely between them, their personalities were unsuited. Maggie wore a perpetually
dour expression, made worse by the realization that
she would never have the man she loved.

''I feel sorry for her,'' Karen said. ''I think she
really did care for Caleb. I know she was distraught
at the funeral.''

''Would she have tried to ruin him for not marrying
her?''

''No,'' Karen said slowly. ''She might go after me,
but never Caleb. I was the one she blamed for destroying her chances with him.''

Grady's expression turned thoughtful. ''Then she
could be seeking revenge on you now,'' he suggested.

''But why? Caleb's gone. What does she have to
gain?''

''She might still be hoping for some sense of satisfaction that she was right all along, that you were
wrong for Caleb and that she would have been the
better choice,'' Grady said.

''I suppose,'' Karen said, but it didn't ring true.

"But that wouldn't explain the earlier incidents. Remember, those happened before Caleb died."

"What about Maggie's father? Would he have wanted to get even with Caleb for spoiling his plan for uniting the two families?"

"Possibly," Karen admitted, though she had a difficult time imagining either of the Fletchers deliberately trying to sabotage her cattle. "Let's think about the Oldhams for a minute. There was a feud between them and the Hansons a zillion years ago. Something about water rights, I think."

"Is it still going on?"

She shook her head. "It was settled ages ago. They have access to the creek that flows through our property. Caleb's grandfather wrote up the agreement himself."

"But if they had this land, the issue could never come up again, right?"

"True."

"I'll visit them tomorrow," Grady said. "Maybe they don't want to take a chance that you might renege on the agreement."

"If you go, I'm coming with you," Karen insisted. "This is my ranch that's being targeted."

"Fine. We'll go right after we get the chores done in the morning."

Once again, Grady's assumption that the chores were his to share took her aback. At the same time, it gave her a warm feeling in the pit of her stomach to know that she was no longer facing everything— not the daily grind, not the battle to keep the ranch afloat—alone.

Grady rubbed a hand across his face. "It's late. I'd better get out of here."

Karen considered offering to let him stay in the guest room, the room they had almost shared earlier, but thought better of it. Her resolve where Grady was concerned was weak enough. It wasn't fair to keep putting him in the position of having to hold back whenever their hormones got the better of them. She couldn't let him stay here until she was ready to let him share her bed.

"It's a long drive," she said eventually. "How about another cup of coffee before you head out?"

He shook his head. "I'll be fine, and the sooner I go, the more rest I'll get, and the sooner I can get back here in the morning."

She walked him to the door. He reached out and cupped the back of her head, then bent to kiss her gently on the forehead. "We're going to get to the bottom of this. I promise you."

But then what? she wondered when he had left. Was he only helping her to solve the puzzle, to tie up loose ends, so that the land would be free and clear of problems when he got his hands on it? That was possible, she told herself. Even likely. And yet, somehow she could no longer make herself believe it.

If discovering that she had feelings for Grady had surprised her, if the depth of her desire for him had startled her, then the discovery that she trusted him was the most shocking thing of all. Feelings—lust— had nothing to do with common sense or logic. They were matters of the heart.

But trust, especially when it involved an old enemy, required more. It meant that both her heart and her head had examined the facts and found Grady Blackhawk trustworthy.

But what if you're wrong? a tiny voice in her head

demanded. *What if Grady is simply sneakier and more clever than you ever imagined?*

Then she would pay a terrible price in guilt and self-recriminations, she concluded. But it was her decision to make, not the Hansons', not even Caleb's.

And the bottom line was that she had learned to trust her instincts where Grady was concerned. He might want her ranch, but he was not the one out to hurt her.

Someone was, though, and she intended to find out who.

Though the prospect was very distasteful to her, Karen called Caleb's parents in Arizona first thing in the morning. They knew more about the old feud between the Oldhams and the Hansons than she did. They also knew more about the high hopes Maggie Fletcher had had where Caleb was concerned.

When Caleb's father answered the phone, she couldn't hide her relief. He would give her straight, thoughtful answers, not a diatribe against Grady, which was all she could have expected from Mrs. Hanson.

"This is old news, but I assume you've got a reason for asking about it," Carl Hanson said.

"There's been another incident," Karen told him. "The fence along the highway was deliberately cut this week."

"That's a pretty obvious place for a person who wanted to do any real damage, don't you think? You were bound to spot the problem."

That hadn't occurred to Karen before, but he was right. Anyone hoping to cause a serious loss of her herd would have cut the fence in some place less likely to be discovered until it was too late.

"What do you think that means? Was it just a warning?"

"Or maybe some kids up to mischief," he suggested.

"If this was the only thing, maybe," she said thoughtfully. "But coupled with the incidents in the past, I don't think so."

"Could have been it was meant to throw suspicion on Grady, so they wanted you to find it right off," he said.

"That makes sense," she agreed. "But who would gain anything by that? Has anyone else ever expressed interest in buying the ranch? Are the Oldhams in any position to buy it to protect the water rights?"

"Not unless they've had a sudden windfall," he said. "Besides, that agreement worked out years ago is airtight. They don't have anything to worry about."

"What about Maggie Fletcher?" Karen asked reluctantly.

Caleb's father sighed. "Ah, yes, Maggie. Now there's a sad situation. Her father was expecting her to pair up with Caleb. He wanted to see the two ranches joined. I don't know which of them was more disappointed when Caleb chose you. I know her father blamed her, told her she wasn't woman enough to catch Caleb. I always thought the way he treated her was downright cruel."

"Would she hate me enough to try to ruin the ranch?"

"*She* wouldn't, but that father of hers is another story. I wouldn't put anything past Jack Fletcher. I told Caleb to keep an eye on him when those last incidents took place, but you know my son. He didn't want to believe it. More likely, he just wanted to believe Grady was behind it.''

This wasn't the first time that Karen had gotten the feeling that the animosity between Caleb and Grady ran deeper than one man's desire to own land belonging to the other.

''Was there more going on between Caleb and Grady than I know about?'' she asked.

Mr. Hanson hesitated. ''I don't know what you mean.''

''The feelings and bitterness seemed to run awfully deep, at least on Caleb's part. Was it just about the ranch?''

''The ranch is the only thing I know about,'' Caleb's father insisted, but something in his voice suggested he was holding back.

That false note lingered in her head long after she'd hung up the phone. When Grady arrived, she poured him a cup of coffee before he could protest, then gestured toward a chair.

''I need to get to the bottom of something,'' she said as he regarded her warily.

''Okay.''

''How well did you and Caleb know each other?''

''We didn't,'' Grady said tersely.

''Oh, come on. You must have. I know you contacted him more than once about buying the ranch.''

''That doesn't mean I knew him, just that I had my lawyer make repeated inquiries.''

She regarded him skeptically. ''You never even met?''

''Never.''

''But he hated you,'' she said. ''Hate that deep

doesn't come from some intellectual dispute over a piece of land.''

''Some people are passionate about what's theirs,'' Grady countered.

She studied him intently. ''There's something you're not telling me, isn't there? You're as tight-lipped about this as Carl Hanson.''

He regarded her with surprise but not dismay. ''You asked him about this?''

''Just this morning. He wouldn't answer me, either.''

''No, I imagine he wouldn't,'' Grady said, his expression wry.

''What's *that* supposed to mean?''

''Can't you drop this? It's not important. If Caleb had wanted you to know, he would have shared it with you. The same with Carl.''

''Well, you're here and they're not,'' she said with a hint of exasperation. ''Tell me, Grady. Why did my husband have it in for you? Why was he so determined that you not get this land?''

''That's easy,'' he said, though he didn't meet her gaze. ''Because it was his and he was possessive.''

''You're talking about the land, but it went beyond that. I can see it in your eyes.''

''You're imagining things.''

Karen lost patience. ''Dammit, Grady, tell me. Was it about a woman? Did you and Caleb fight over some woman?''

Grady sighed heavily. ''Not the way you mean,'' he said finally. ''And it wasn't me.''

''You're talking in riddles,'' she accused.

His lips curved slightly at that. ''Apparently it's a

family trait. My grandfather does that, too, when he doesn't want to answer a question.''

"Well, I intend to keep coming back to this one until you give me a straight answer,'' she said. "So why not get it over with?''

"Okay,'' he said with obvious reluctance. "This was about my father and Anna Hanson.''

Stunned, Karen stared at him. "Caleb's mother?''

He nodded.

"But how? When? Before she married Carl?''

"No, unfortunately, it was much later. They almost ran off together.''

Karen couldn't seem to take it in. "Anna Hanson almost abandoned her family to run away with your father?''

"They would have left, if my father hadn't been killed in an accident on his way to get her. He was late because he had stopped to try to explain to me why he wouldn't be home. She blamed me for his death. It's irrational, I know, but she couldn't blame herself.''

"My God,'' Karen whispered. "And Caleb knew?''

Grady nodded. "He knew. He'd seen them together, and he found her bags packed on the night of the accident.''

"What about Carl?''

"He knew as well, but he acted as if nothing had happened. For the sake of his pride, I suppose, he pretended that Anna had never had any intention of going anywhere with my father. He and Anna just went along with their marriage.''

Karen thought about her husband, about the occasional dark looks he had cast at his mother, about the tension that sometimes flared between him and his father. He'd never been able to bring himself to blame either of them for the choices they had made back then, and Charlie Blackhawk was dead, so he had blamed Grady, instead. All of that anger and hurt had been directed at the only person who'd been as innocent of blame as Caleb himself had been.

"What about your mother?" Karen asked Grady. "How did she take all of this?"

His expression turned grim. "She wasn't as good at pretending. She turned to alcohol. I don't think she had a sober minute for ten years before it finally caught up with her and she died."

"How old were you when she died?"

"Nineteen."

"Which means you were only nine when all of this happened?"

He nodded.

"And Caleb was thirteen?"

"An age when a boy is all caught up in his own raging hormones and doesn't want to think about his parents as sexual beings. He certainly doesn't want to think of his mother wanting to be with a man other than his father in that way."

"But to blame you," Karen said. "How could he?"

"It wasn't logical, unless you believe the sins of the fathers live on in their sons, though I doubt any of that was on Caleb's mind. I was just an easy target for all that pent-up rage he couldn't express to the people involved."

Pent-up rage, Karen thought, wondering if that had ultimately been the stress that had damaged Caleb's heart. Was it possible that even years later, he had quite literally died of a broken heart?

As saddened as she was by that, she couldn't help being glad that the secret was finally out. It helped her to see everything in a new light. It helped to know that Caleb's judgment of Grady had been so terribly misdirected. Wasn't that what Stella had hinted at so many weeks ago? Obviously she had known the whole story.

Perhaps if Caleb had ever gotten to know the man he considered an enemy, he would have seen that Grady was as much a victim as Caleb himself had been. And the fierce competitiveness and anger that only Caleb had felt might not have contributed to his death.

Chapter Eleven

It was almost noon by the time Grady and Karen were able to drive over to see the Fletchers and Old-hams. They were about to leave when they heard a commotion outside. Grady opened the back door just in time to see Dooley thundering toward the house, his horse at a full gallop. The old man looked mad enough to break a few boards in two with his bare hands. He reined in his horse just a few feet from where Grady and Karen stood.

"Dooley, what is it?" Karen asked, regarding him with alarm. "Where's Hank?"

"I left him in the pasture," he said, casting a worried frown at Grady. "Could I have a word with you?"

"Hold it," Karen commanded. "If you speak to anybody around here, Dooley Jenkins, it'll be me. What's happened? Is Hank okay?"

Dooley's expression turned resigned. "He's fine, but that prize bull you just bought, he's not so good."

Grady saw the color drain out of Karen's face. He put an arm around her waist, but she seemed oblivious to it. He could feel her trembling. This was just one more blow to a woman who'd faced too many of them.

"What happened? Is he sick?" she asked.

"Not sick," Dooley said. "Shot."

Karen gasped. "Shot? By whom? Was it an accident?"

"Not unless you believe people are taking target practice in your pasture and that bull just got in the way," Dooley said with disgust. "Looks to me like somebody took dead aim at him."

"Is he alive?" Grady asked.

"Barely."

"I'll call the vet," Karen said at once, and disappeared inside, her spine straight, her familiar resolve back in place.

When she'd gone, Grady regarded the old man intently. "Any chance he'll make it?"

"Not much of one, if you ask me. Whoever did this knew what he was doing. He got him good. Calling the vet's probably a waste of time and money."

"Still, she has to try or she'll never forgive herself," Grady concluded. "I'll saddle the horses and ride out with her. Can you wait and bring the vet out when he gets here?"

"Will do," Dooley agreed. "Then I want to help you find the son of a bitch who did this. The missus was counting on that bull for breeding. Paid an arm and a leg for him."

"Let's not worry about that now," Grady said

grimly. "I can spare a couple of bulls. I imagine Frank Davis will offer to help out, too, once his son gets wind of this from Cassie." He met Dooley's gaze. "One more thing, from now on Karen doesn't go anywhere on this ranch without one of us with her."

"Got it," Dooley said, his expression somber. "When you're not around, me or Hank will stick close by, no matter how much she grumbles about it."

Grady grinned. "I imagine she'll grumble quite a lot."

Dooley's lips twitched. "Yes, indeed. The woman can't stand to have anybody coddling her. She's dead set on proving she can handle anything that's thrown her way. Been that way ever since Caleb died."

"I doubt she was counting on this, though," Grady said. "From what you say, whoever took aim at that bull was up to no good. I don't want to wait around to see what he has in mind next. I think it's time to get the sheriff involved."

"She won't thank you for that," Dooley said.

Grady figured that was probably an understatement, but he couldn't afford to worry about Karen's reaction. It was more important to keep her safe.

"Once we're gone, can you call and fill him in?" Grady asked.

Dooley chuckled. "If you think having me do the deed will save your hide, you're dead wrong, but I'll do it. Now get those horses saddled before she comes out here and wants to know why the two of us are lollygagging when there's a crisis."

Dooley seemed to be taking to his role as co-conspirator and self-appointed protector even better than Grady had anticipated. He grinned at the old man.

"You're a good person to have around, Dooley."

The old man nodded as if the compliment were his due. "Had my doubts about you, when you first started hanging around here, but you ain't so bad yourself."

"What is this, some kind of mutual admiration society?" Karen demanded when she found them both right where she'd left them. Evidently she'd heard the tail end of their conversation, too. "The vet's on the way. Come on, Grady. I want to get out to that field. Maybe there's something we can do till he gets here."

But there was nothing to be done. By the time they reached Hank, the bull was dead. The hand had tried to stanch the flow of blood with his own shirt, but the effort had been futile.

Her expression devastated, Karen fell to her knees beside the animal and ran her hand over his blood-soaked chest. "Damn whoever did this," she whispered, tears streaming down her cheeks. "I don't care if it was an accident."

The last was muttered as if she were clinging desperately to an explanation she could understand.

Grady glanced at Hank, who subtly shook his head, confirming Dooley's opinion as well. Grady studied the massive beast and saw what the two men had seen, three distinct wounds. One shot might have been an accident, but three? Not a chance.

Grady glanced up at the sound of hooves pounding across the field. Looked as if Dooley had been successful in getting the sheriff out here in record time, right along with the veterinarian, whose services were no longer needed.

Karen rose stiffly from the ground, her complexion pale, bright patches of color in her cheeks and a flash of anger in her eyes. Surprise streaked across her face when she spotted the sheriff.

"Michael, what are you doing here?" she asked as if it weren't perfectly obvious that someone had alerted him.

"Dooley called me. Said there was a problem."

"Some fool accidentally shot my new bull," she said.

"It wasn't an accident," Grady said quietly, ignoring the protest forming on Karen's lips.

"Oh?" Michael Dunn said, stepping close to examine the animal. "Three bullet wounds. You're right, Blackhawk. That's no accident."

He glanced at Karen. "Why don't you tell me what else has been going on out here? I understand there have been a few other incidents."

Karen scowled at Dooley, then turned back to the sheriff. "Nothing serious. Some fence was cut."

"And an unexpected outbreak of a virus in our herd," Dooley added pointedly. "That was about a year ago, along with another section of fence destroyed. And a fire that burned out most of the pasture."

"Any idea who's behind it?" Michael asked, his gaze subtly shifting toward Grady.

"Not me, if that's what you're thinking," Grady told him.

"It's no secret that you want this land."

"I imagine it's no secret that I've also offered to buy it, fair and square."

"That's true," Karen said.

"But you turned him down, am I right?" the sheriff persisted.

"Yes, but—"

Michael cut Karen's protest off in midsentence. "Which means he has an excellent motive for pulling a few stunts that might make you change your mind," he concluded.

"Don't you dare jump to such a ridiculous conclusion," Karen snapped. "Grady is not behind this. Besides, he was with me when the bull was shot."

"He could have paid someone to do that," the sheriff countered.

"Then why would he tell me to call you?" Dooley demanded, shrugging when Grady scowled at him. "Better to have her getting all worked up over you insisting on getting the sheriff than having you hauled off to jail, because the sheriff's got his facts wrong."

"Maybe, maybe not," Grady said, when Karen whirled on him.

"You're the one who got the sheriff out here?" she demanded.

"Not technically," Grady said, then conceded, "But it was my idea."

"And a really brilliant one, don't you think?" she snapped. "Couldn't you see that this was exactly what would happen?"

"Actually I thought the sheriff might be a bit more open-minded," he said with a pointed look at Michael.

"Oh, for goodness' sake, when has a law enforcement officer ever been open-minded? He wants to solve the case as quickly as possible, period."

Michael winced. "Usually we prefer to nail the right suspect," he corrected.

"Couldn't prove that by me," Karen said. "Not based on the last ten minutes, anyway."

Michael sighed. "Why don't we all go back to the house and talk this through rationally?"

"What an absolutely brilliant plan," Karen said sarcastically.

Grady grinned at her. "Darlin', I think you've won. You might want to be a bit more gracious about it."

She scowled at him. "I'm not feeling especially gracious at the moment. In fact, I'm mad enough to knock a few heads together."

"Any heads in particular?"

"Besides yours?" she inquired sweetly. "And Dooley's and Michael's?"

"I'd say that about covers it," Grady said, grinning at her.

"This is not the least bit amusing, Grady Blackhawk."

His expression sobered at once. "The situation? No, not at all. But you? You are something else."

Her frown deepened. "Don't even go there. One word about how cute I am when I'm angry, and you're going to be as dead as that poor old bull."

Dooley guffawed, then covered his mouth and looked away.

Karen whirled on him. "I'd watch it, if I were you. You're next on my list."

"Me? What did I do?" Dooley asked, looking hurt.

"You got the sheriff out here."

"Somebody had to," he said flatly. "Grady was right. It was time."

Grady touched her cheek. "You know it was," he said quietly.

She heaved a heartfelt sigh, then nodded. "Maybe so, but I don't have to like it."

"No, darlin'," he agreed sympathetically. "You definitely don't have to like it."

After the morning she'd had, she was pretty much entitled to hate the world.

Karen couldn't seem to hold on to anything. She dropped the coffee mugs on the floor, shattering one of them. When Grady brushed aside her attempts to clean it up and did it himself, she tried to get the coffee grinds into the coffeemaker, only to spill most of them on the counter.

Tears stung her eyes when Grady put his hand over hers.

"Sit down," he said. "I'll make the coffee. You need to get some food into you. It's way past lunchtime."

"I can't eat. I have to do something," she said, her voice catching. "If I don't, I'll fall apart. This was the final straw. I am never going to be able to keep this place now."

"Of course, you are, if that's what you want," he insisted.

"I can't afford to replace that bull."

"Insurance will cover the cost."

She shook her head. "I had to let it lapse."

"Then I'll bring over a couple of my bulls, or Frank Davis can bring over one of his. Cole will insist on it."

"I don't want Cassie dragging Cole or her father-in-law into this. And I don't want to rely on you any more than I have already."

"This is an emergency, and folks around here help

each other out. You know that. You'd do the same
for a neighbor if he needed help.''

''Yes, of course, but—''

''No buts,'' he said. ''Now I would suggest you
cut the sheriff a piece of that apple pie you baked
yesterday, but I'm not sure you ought to be handling
a knife at the moment.''

''Very amusing,'' she said, already reaching for a
plate and a knife.

She managed that task with no further disasters,
probably because she was going about it in slow motion just to prove Grady wrong. She put the pie in
front of Michael, then began pacing.

''Sit down,'' the sheriff suggested.

''I can't. I'm too jumpy.''

''Okay, then, why don't you begin at the beginning
and tell me what's been going on out here.''

Karen gave him the short version, leaving out all
of her suspicions about the neighbors. Grady, unfortunately, wasn't so reticent. He laid out every piece
of information they'd discussed about old grudges
and recent jealousy. Michael nodded when he was
finished.

''Okay, then, I'll see what I can find out.'' He regarded Grady with a pointed look. ''You stay out of
it. This is an official investigation now. I don't want
a couple of amateurs nosing around.''

''Whatever you say,'' Grady agreed.

Karen kept her mouth clamped shut, since she
didn't want to lie straight to the sheriff's face. There
was no way she was going to stay out of this. That
was her bull lying dead out there, her ranch that was
under attack.

"I didn't hear any agreement from you," Michael said, his gaze leveled on her.

"I understand what you're saying," she said.

Michael's gaze narrowed. "That's not quite the same thing as saying you'll leave this investigation to me, now, is it?"

"Not quite," she said cheerfully. "How clever of you to see that." Actually, she was surprised that he'd caught the subtle distinction.

"Karen, I'm warning you," he said, his expression grim. "Stay out of it."

"I hear you," she said again.

He sighed heavily, then turned to Grady. "Keep her from meddling in this. If she starts asking a lot of questions, whoever's behind this just might decide that she's a threat."

Grady nodded. "I'll do what I can. I won't let her out of my sight for a minute."

Michael seemed to conclude that that was the most satisfying answer he was likely to get. "I'll be in touch," he said.

The minute he was gone, Karen reached for her jacket.

"Where do you think you're going?" Grady demanded. "You heard what the sheriff said."

"And you heard what I said—or, rather, what I didn't say. I'm going to see Maggie Fletcher. And once I've had a chat with her, then I'm going to see the Oldhams, just the way we planned. Are you coming with me or not?"

"Is there any way I can talk you out of this?" Grady asked.

He reached out and caressed her cheek, his gaze intent. "Maybe persuade you to rethink your plan?"

His touch raised goose bumps, but she managed to shake her head. "No," she said flatly. "There's nothing you can say or do to stop me."

With a resigned sigh, he reached for his coat. "Let's go, then. I just hope we don't bump straight into the sheriff ten minutes after he warned us both to stay out of his way."

"He'll be going to the Oldhams. They're closest. That's why we're going to see Maggie."

"And you don't think we'll cross paths on the highway?"

"As long as we're on the highway and not in her driveway, he won't be able to prove a thing," she said airily.

Grady chuckled. "You have a much more devious mind than I'd ever imagined. I like it."

For the first time all morning, a grin tugged at her lips. "I knew there was some reason you were sticking around."

"Oh, believe me, darlin', there are a lot of reasons I'm here," he said, his gaze locked with hers. "That's not even close to the top of the list."

Karen swallowed hard at that. She wanted desperately to ask about that list, but now wasn't the time. Later, though, she intended to find out what—besides her land—would keep a man like Grady interested in her.

Maggie Fletcher looked exhausted. Her normally ruddy complexion had a gray cast to it. Her short hair was mussed, as if she'd been running her fingers through it in a nervous gesture for hours, if not days. Her eyes, which Grady recalled as a vibrant, glowing amber color, were listless, though they sparked a bit brighter when she spotted Karen emerging from Grady's truck.

"What are you doing here?" she demanded ungraciously, ignoring Grady completely to focus on Karen.

"We need to talk," Karen said.

"Why?" Maggie asked, not bothering to hide her hostility.

"Because of Caleb."

Unmistakable pain darkened Maggie's eyes before the sparks came back livelier than ever. "I will not discuss Caleb with you. It's because of you he's dead."

Karen winced, but she didn't back down. "I'm sorry you feel that way."

"It's the truth," Maggie said.

Grady saw Karen's shoulders sag at Maggie's refusal to back down from the accusation, but again she stood her ground.

"I know you cared for him," she said gently.

"I loved him," Maggie said fiercely. "He and I would have been perfect for each other. That was the way it was meant to be." Years of bitterness came boiling out as she hurled hateful comment after hateful comment at Karen. "You killed him. Instead of helping him, you drove him into an early grave with your demands."

"I made no demands on Caleb," Karen said. "It was his choice to work as hard as he did to save the ranch. That land meant the world to him."

"But nothing to you," Maggie accused. "He told me you hated it, that you asked him to sell."

Karen reeled at that. She reached out for support,

but there was nothing there. Grady took a step closer and she latched on to his arm.

"I didn't," she whispered. "I never asked him to sell. If he told you that, it was a lie."

"Oh, really?" Maggie shot back, her tone scathing. "Then why are you with *him?*" She glanced pointedly at Grady. "Everyone knows he wants that land. I'm sure you can't wait to take his money and go off on one of those trips you were always going on and on about. Do you know how guilty it made Caleb feel that he couldn't take you?"

Karen faltered. Her cheeks turned pale. "I...I need to sit down."

"Then get into your fancy truck and leave," Maggie said. "There's no place for you here."

For an instant, Grady thought Karen might argue, might insist on asking all of the questions she'd had no chance to direct at Maggie, but she didn't. Looking defeated, she turned toward the truck. He saw that she was safely tucked inside and that the heater was working, before walking back to Maggie himself.

"Just how much time were you and Caleb spending together while he was married to another woman?" Grady inquired. "Were you having an affair, the way you clearly want Karen to believe? Or is that just some spiteful suggestion you wanted to plant in her head to add to her grief?"

Maggie's expression faltered.

"I thought so," he said. "You're a cruel woman, Maggie Fletcher. It's little wonder that Caleb chose a woman like Karen over you."

He turned on his heel and headed for the truck.

"Damn you, Grady Blackhawk," Maggie shouted after him. "And you, too, Mrs. High-and-Mighty

Hanson. I hope you wind up in the ground right next to Caleb, and the sooner the better!"

When Grady got into the truck, he took a deep breath before facing Karen. She was visibly trembling, her composure shattered.

"I had no idea," she whispered.

"It was all lies," Grady told her. "Caleb wasn't spending time with her, sharing secrets with her."

"I know that," Karen said dismissively, as if the notion had never crossed her mind. "I had no idea she was so angry, so bitter. I knew she resented me, but this..." She shuddered.

Grady reached for her icy hands, clasping them in his until he felt the warmth return.

"She could be the one, Grady. She's angry enough to do all of those things, even to have killed that bull."

"If we can see that, Michael will see it as well. Let him deal with her."

"Oh, you can be sure I won't be coming back here," Karen reassured him.

"Good, because she's just unstable enough to try to hurt you in some misguided attempt at seeking justice for Caleb's death."

"She wouldn't go that far," Karen said, but she didn't sound nearly as certain as she might have an hour ago.

"It's not a chance you can take," Grady insisted. "Steer clear of her. At the very least, she needs some help."

Karen sighed and turned to look out the window. She was huddled by the door, looking more dejected than she had since he'd first seen her at Caleb's funeral.

Making a sudden decision, Grady turned the truck toward Winding River. Karen barely seemed to notice, which only confirmed his opinion that she needed something drastic to cheer her up. And she needed food. There was one place where she could get both—Stella's.

Karen seemed oblivious to everything until they approached the outskirts of town. She blinked then, and turned to him.

"What are we doing here?"

"We're going out to dinner at Stella's. It's meat loaf night. Any objections?"

"No," she said dispiritedly.

As soon as they walked into the restaurant, he caught Cassie's eye. As Karen headed straight for the booth in the back, he called Cassie aside.

"Can you get Gina, Cole and anybody else you can think of in here for dinner? Karen's had a rough day. She needs some friendly faces and lively conversation."

Cassie nodded without the slightest hesitation. Nor did she ask a lot of unnecessary questions. It was apparently enough that her friend needed help.

"Emma's in town, too. I'll have them here in fifteen minutes and Stella can take over for me." She studied Grady intently. "You really care about her, don't you?"

Grady wasn't entirely comfortable discussing his feelings, not when he hadn't fully analyzed them himself yet. But the expression on Cassie's face showed none of the disapproval or suspicion he might have anticipated.

"Yeah," he admitted. "I care about her."

"Good," Cassie said with an approving nod. "That way the rest of us won't have to kill you."

He chuckled. "Well, there's a relief all the way around."

She grinned. "Isn't it, though. Now go on back. Reinforcements will be here soon."

"You're a good friend, you know," he said gratefully.

"Yes," she agreed. "But so are you. And isn't it nice that she has so many of us?"

Grady was surprised at just how comforting he found that fact. He'd always been pretty much a loner, and had always been able to convince himself that he didn't need anyone, except maybe his grandfather.

But as he watched first Gina, then Emma and finally Cole and Cassie slide into chairs around the big table at the back of Stella's, as he saw the beginnings of a smile tremble on Karen's lips, then finally heard the sound of her laughter, for the first time ever he regretted not being part of a larger circle of friends himself.

Chapter Twelve

For a day that had begun so traumatically, it was moving toward an amazingly happy conclusion. Karen looked around the table at Stella's and felt a familiar warmth steal through her. She'd been surprised when first Gina and then Emma had shown up, even more startled when Cole and Cassie had joined them, then she had caught the conspiratorial wink between Cassie and Grady and known that he was responsible for gathering her friends together just when she needed them the most.

She reached for his hand. "Thank you," she whispered in his ear.

He faced her with an unbelievably innocent look. "For what?"

"For knowing exactly what I needed," she told him. "And for making it happen."

"I just spoke to Cassie," he said, shrugging it off as if it had been no big deal.

"And told her I'd had a lousy day," Karen added.

He looked embarrassed at being given credit for something so simple. "Something like that. She did the rest."

"You're an amazingly thoughtful man, Grady," she said, even though it was evident the praise was making him uncomfortable. "It couldn't have been easy. You had to wonder how they'd feel about you being here with me."

"Because they were all friends of Caleb's," he said flatly. "Yeah, well, I figured I could handle whatever cross-examinations they cared to dish out. So far, they've been fairly restrained."

"I imagine Cassie warned them off because she didn't want me any more upset than I was when I came in here. Now that my mood's improved, though, watch out." She glanced across the table, grinned and told him in a conspiratorial tone, "Emma's getting that gleam in her eyes, the one she gets right before she destroys a witness."

He followed the direction of her gaze to check out the attorney, who was indeed regarding him with a speculative expression and a worrisome hint of distrust.

"I think I'll go make a few calls," he said, clearly anxious to duck out.

"Oh, no, you don't," Karen said. "I don't want her thinking you're a coward."

"Not a coward, just cautious. I don't want to ruin the mood by telling your friend to mind her own business. She might take offense."

Karen chuckled. "If you think that's going to faze

her, you're crazy. Emma thinks everything is her business, especially if it affects one of us. Now sit here and face the music. I'll protect you."

"So, Grady," Emma began, leaning toward him, "how did you happen to be at the ranch when Karen got the news about her bull being shot?"

"We had some plans," Karen said, hoping to waylay that part of the inevitable interrogation.

Of course, that was exactly the wrong thing to say. The glint in Emma's eyes brightened. "Oh, really? What sort of plans?"

Karen was about to respond, when Grady laid a hand over hers and shook his head.

"I can handle this," he said, then turned to Emma. "We were going to pay a few calls on Karen's neighbors."

That seemed to disconcert Emma completely. "Why?" she asked, her expression baffled.

"Just to chat," Grady said cheerfully. "Haven't you ever dropped by to pay a neighborly visit?"

"Well, of course, but the two of you, together..." Her gaze narrowed. "What's going on? Were you counting on Karen to smoothe the way for you so the neighbors would accept you once you've stolen her ranch from her?"

Grady sighed. "I'm not stealing anything. As an attorney, surely you know the inadvisability of making slanderous accusations."

Emma refused to back down, just as Karen had predicted. She merely leaned forward, her gaze intimidating, and said, "If the shoe fits, Mr. Blackhawk."

"It doesn't," he said mildly. "Which brings us back to being careful about the words you choose to describe a legitimate business offer."

"Then you still want the ranch," Emma concluded.

"Of course. That hasn't changed."

She glanced at Karen. "And you're still refusing to sell?"

"So far," Karen said, determined to match Grady's light tone.

"Then it seems to me as if your continued presence at the ranch constitutes harassment," Emma said to Grady.

When a dull flush crept into Grady's cheeks, Karen concluded enough was enough. "Okay, that's it," Karen advised her friend. "Grady is not harassing me. He's helping me to figure out who's behind all of the attempts to ruin me."

Her announcement was greeted by a collective gasp.

"What attempts?" Gina demanded. "And why haven't you said anything about this to us?"

"I didn't think they amounted to anything, at least not until today."

Cole turned to Grady. "But you disagree? These are serious?" he asked.

Grady nodded. "Serious enough. Cut fence lines, an infection deliberately spread to her herd and today somebody shot the bull she was counting on for breeding."

"Damn," Cole muttered, then looked at Karen. "No need to worry about that. I'll speak to my father. He just bought a prize bull for stud. I'm sure he'll work something out with you."

"Thank you. Grady's already volunteered to bring over a couple of bulls from his herd."

Emma continued to regard Grady with suspicion. "Why would you do that?"

His gaze never wavered from hers. "Why wouldn't I?"

"I'm sure you'd rather see her go bankrupt," Emma accused.

"You're wrong," Grady said flatly. "At this point, the only thing I care about is keeping her safe."

Emma regarded him with shock. "You think Karen's in danger?"

"Whoever shot that bull was making a statement," Grady said. "So, yes, I think she could be in danger."

"Then you'll move in with us, Karen," Cassie said at once.

"Absolutely," Cole agreed.

Karen sighed at the rush of protectiveness. "Thank you, but I'm not going anywhere. I'll be just fine at the ranch. The whole purpose of this is to chase me away. I won't give in to that."

"Her hands and I will see that nothing happens to her," Grady added.

"The hands will be in the bunkhouse, and you'll be in the next county," Cassie pointed out.

Grady's gaze clashed with hers. "No," he said. "Until this is resolved, I'll be at the ranch."

Karen's mouth gaped at the unexpected declaration. This was a turn of events she definitely hadn't anticipated. "You will?"

"Oh, no," Emma said. "You're not using this to get your foot in the door out there."

"Oh, Emma, be quiet," Karen snapped. "This is between Grady and me."

"But—" Emma began.

"Emma, I said I would handle it," Karen said pointedly, ignoring the stunned expressions around the table. She touched Grady's cheek. "I appreciate what you're trying to do, I really do, but it's not necessary. Once we tell the sheriff about our conversation with Maggie, I'm sure it won't be long before he brings her in for questioning."

"There's no guarantee he'll arrest her," Grady argued. "Nor do we know for certain that she's behind this. We only know how deep her bitterness toward you runs."

Gina held up a hand. "Hold it. Are we talking about Maggie Fletcher?"

Karen nodded.

"You think she's behind all of this?" Gina asked, her expression incredulous.

"It's possible," Karen said cautiously. "She wasn't happy about me marrying Caleb. And this morning she made it abundantly clear that she still resents me."

Cole shook his head. "Maggie's not at fault here, not if you're including what happened to the bull," he said. "Maggie couldn't hit a barn at ten paces. She's terrified of guns, has been ever since her daddy got hit by a ricocheting bullet when he was trying to teach her to shoot. That's what ended his rodeo career."

"Oh, my God, I'd forgotten that," Karen said, recalling how the story had circulated through several counties, making Maggie the butt of a barrage of jokes. "You're right. Her aim was so bad that her father declared her a danger to herself and everyone around her. She hasn't picked up a gun since."

"That you know of," Grady said, clearly unwilling to give up their prime suspect so readily. "Maybe she's been practicing."

No one seemed to buy that, Karen included. "That

brings us back to square one,'' she said. ''We have
no idea who's been behind these attacks.''

Grady's grim expression turned determined. ''All
the more reason for me to move in with you until this
is settled.'' He scowled at her. ''Don't even waste
your breath arguing with me.''

Karen didn't intend to try. For once, Emma remained silent as well. And after intense scrutiny of
Karen's face, even Cassie gave up trying to persuade
her to move in with her and Cole.

Grady gave a nod of satisfaction. ''I guess that's
settled then.''

It was settled, all right. What was less certain was
why the decision had set off a surge of anticipation
deep inside Karen. She was pretty sure it had absolutely nothing to do with her sense of security. In fact,
quite the opposite. Having Grady move in represented
a whole new kind of danger.

Grady couldn't pinpoint the precise moment when
his mission had shifted, but there was undeniable
proof that it had. He couldn't be in the same room
with Karen without wanting her, without trying to
seize whatever kisses she was willing to permit him.
He wanted kisses and a whole lot more, which was
just one reason he'd maneuvered his way into staying
at the ranch.

The fact that she hadn't fought him harder suggested that she was accepting his presence, accepting
that there was something incredible happening between them despite all the odds against it.

''I'll need to run out to my place and get a few
things,'' he told her after they'd left Stella's.

She nodded, though her gaze seemed determinedly fixed on the passing scenery.

"You can come along. In fact, I'd feel better if you did. I don't want you alone at your house even for a couple of hours."

She turned a quick glance on him, then turned away again. "I'll be fine," she insisted. "I'll need to tidy up the guest room so it's ready for you."

He grinned at that. She clearly intended that as a message to him curbing any expectations he might have about moving into her room, rather than down the hall. She seemed to have forgotten that that guest room had already been the scene of an incredibly intimate encounter.

"You had any company since we were in there the other day?" he inquired wryly.

A blush bloomed on her cheeks. "No, of course not, but..." Her voice faltered.

"Then I'd say any tidying up can wait. We barely rumpled the sheets."

She frowned at his teasing. "Whose fault was that?"

"I'd have to say it was a mutual decision," he said, grinning at her.

"You'd be wrong," she countered. "You made the decision all on your own, thinking you knew best, just the way you're doing now."

He turned to meet her gaze. "Are you saying you have regrets about the way things turned out?"

"Well, of course, I do, don't you?"

"Speaking from a purely personal perspective, I'd have to say that night's been on my mind a lot."

"Would you have changed the outcome?" she persisted, her gaze now clashing with his.

Grady thought about it, thought about how he'd been aching to make love to her for a long time now, but eventually he shook his head. "No, I can't say that I would."

Her eyes widened in obvious surprise. "You wouldn't?"

"Despite all these claims you're uttering now, you weren't ready to accept me into your life, much less into your bed. We made the right decision." He reached for her hand, lifted it to his lips. "But we can certainly reconsider it."

She gave a little nod at that. "I think we should." Her heated gaze locked with his. "In fact, why don't you forget that trip out to your place, so we can reconsider it right now."

Worried that the traumatic day had simply made her vulnerable, he searched her face, but he didn't see a single trace of lingering doubts. Grady had already passed the turnoff to the Hanson ranch, but he slammed on the brakes and turned the truck around.

Ten minutes later, he'd pulled to a stop by her house. Still clinging to the steering wheel, he faced straight ahead, not daring to look at her.

"Have you changed your mind?" he asked, giving her one last chance to back out.

"No," she said, her voice strong and not the least bit uncertain.

"Thank heaven," he murmured, leaping out of the truck and going around to catch her in his arms. He scooped her off her feet and twirled her around until they were both dizzy.

"Grady, you're crazy," she chided, laughing. "Put me down."

"Not until I can put you down on that big, old bed," he said, and headed for the house.

As if she weighed nothing, he climbed the stairs eagerly, two at a time. Her twinkling eyes met his. "If I didn't know better, Grady Blackhawk, I'd think you were as anxious as a bridegroom on his wedding night."

His step almost faltered at the image, but he managed a grin. The idea wasn't nearly as repugnant as it should have been. He'd never given much thought to marriage or happily-ever-after, but if ever a woman could turn his thoughts in that direction, it was surely Karen.

Inside the guest bedroom, where late afternoon sun had cast a pale glow across everything, he gently deposited her on top of the colorful old patchwork quilt.

"Not being all that familiar with wedding nights," he said, studying her closely, "I can't say for certain, but you seem to me to have the radiant glow of a bride yourself."

"That's how I feel," she admitted in a whisper. Her eyes swam with unshed tears. "Oh, Grady, how did this happen? I never expected it, not in a million years."

"I didn't either," he told her candidly. "But I don't regret it. Do you?"

"No," she said fervently. "How could I, when I feel so incredibly alive?"

"Oh, darlin', just you wait," he said as he stripped off his boots and shirt, then joined her on the bed.

He cradled her in his arms, giving both of them time to adjust, time to prepare for the step they were taking. He knew that despite all her brave declarations, Karen was still harboring doubts. How could she not? She had loved her husband, a man who had considered Grady his enemy, even if that thinking had been the irrational bitterness of a boy carried over into adulthood. Grady understood all of that, which made the fact that Karen was with him all the more precious.

He stroked her cheek, rubbed the pad of his thumb across her lower lip, felt the heat begin to rise in her…and in him. Her soft moan was too much, an invitation for the kiss he'd been deliberately postponing.

When his mouth settled over hers, tasting, savoring, coaxing, she responded with more abandon than she ever had before, her lips parting, her tongue sweeping across his lips. She moved restlessly beside him, an invitation for more adventurous exploration.

Beneath the wool of her sweater, her skin was hot and soft as silk. Inch by tempting inch, he slid the sweater higher, pressing kisses in its wake until she trembled. Impatient now, she ripped the sweater over her head and tossed it aside, but when she would have unclasped her bra, Grady stopped her.

"Not just yet," he said, his gaze feasting on the swell of breasts concealed by plain white no-nonsense cotton. Somehow that image seemed to epitomize Karen, a devastating mix of fiery sensuality and practicality.

He ran a finger along the edge of the fabric, where pale skin burned beneath his touch. He skimmed a caress across her nipple, which thrust against the soft fabric. When he could stand it no longer, he bent and drew that hard, tight bud into his mouth, feeling the shudder that washed over her.

"You're torturing me, you know that, don't you?" she whispered on a gasp.

"Am I?" He was delighted by the admission.

"You needn't sound so pleased with yourself," she grumbled, then reached for the snap on his jeans. She had it open and the zipper down before he could prevent it.

And then she was touching him, adding to the pulsing heat of his arousal, sending him closer to the edge than he wanted to be.

"Clever woman," he said, shifting out of her reach. "But not just yet. We have places to go and things to try before we get to that point."

"Oh, really?" She seemed intrigued with that. "Tell me."

He shook his head. "I'll show you."

He resumed the concentrated attention to her breasts, finally taking off the bra and circling each tight peak with his tongue before drawing it into his mouth. Her hips bucked as he took her closer and closer to release just with that slow, suckling assault on her senses.

Satisfied that he'd distracted her, he slid off her shoes and jeans, then began working his way up silky calf and rounded thigh with kisses meant to tease and torment. She was writhing when he slipped his fingers beneath her panties and found her slick and ready. One wicked caress, then two, and she was coming apart, her eyes wide with surprise as waves of pleasure washed over her.

"Not fair," she accused when she finally caught her breath.

"Oh, darlin', it's not over. We're just getting started."

To prove it, he shucked his jeans and jockey shorts, retrieved a condom from his wallet, then started once again to coax her toward a whole new peak.

This time he allowed her clever, wicked hands to roam where she wished until at last, knowing his restraint was at the breaking point, he poised above her parted legs. Their gazes locked, he slowly entered her, withdrew, then thrust deeper into that welcoming heat.

With each thrust, her hips rose to meet him, as her flushed skin turned slick with sweat. When he pressed a kiss to the pulse at the base of her throat, it was thundering, as was his.

Her name was on his lips when the explosion tore through him, his shudders setting off hers, rippling through both of them for what seemed an eternity, until at last they faded into quiet, exhausted satisfaction.

He rolled onto his back, taking her with him, holding her as if she were the most precious, fragile gift he'd ever been given, though he knew she would never, ever appreciate being considered anything but strong. This…everything about her…was amazing.

And then he felt a drop of moisture fall from her face onto his. One quick glance told the story: These weren't happy tears. Though she quickly, impatiently tried to brush them away, it was too late. He had seen the truth. They were tears of regret and sorrow.

Grady felt his heart break in two. How could she regret anything so perfect?

It was Caleb, of course. Always Caleb. Grady had to wonder, would there ever come a day when Caleb Hanson *didn't* share a bed with them?

Chapter Thirteen

Grady had seen her tears, felt them, Karen realized as she lay in his arms. She felt the sudden stirring of tension, saw the distance in his eyes where only moments ago there had been such fiery passion.

When he eased away from her, then turned his back, she felt as if she had betrayed two men, not one.

Eventually she slid out of bed and went to her own room, where she showered as if that could wipe away not just the evidence of their lovemaking but her regrets as well.

How could she have been so wrong? she wondered. She'd been so sure she was ready, that her feelings for Grady ran deep enough for this next step in their relationship.

And they did, dammit. She had felt alive and treasured when he'd been making love to her. She had responded in a way she never had with Caleb, without any inhibitions at all.

"Oh, God, that's it," she murmured, burying her face in her pillow. It wasn't just that awful sense of having betrayed someone that she'd been feeling, but guilt that she had felt more, given more, with Grady Blackhawk than she ever had with the man she'd married.

The passion she had shared with Caleb had been quieter, less intense, comfortable—what a terrible word, she thought—even at the beginning. They had been perfectly matched, no extreme lows or giddy highs, just steady, *comfortable* companions, partners in the running of the ranch.

There was nothing easy or comfortable about Grady. He was a man who tested the limits, who demanded responses that reached new heights. She'd just experienced one of those amazing, astonishing highs. Now, alone in her own bed, she was crashing to its opposite low.

"I can't do this," she whispered aloud.

Being with Grady put her at risk, rocked her emotionally in a way she wasn't prepared to handle. She was afraid to trust this new passion, afraid the fire would burn itself out and she'd be left with nothing.

It had happened before. She had lost Caleb, the man she had expected to spend her entire life with. And if solid, dependable Caleb could leave her, then what guarantee did she have that a volatile man like Grady might not as well, in one way or another? She wasn't sure she could survive another loss. Or the discovery that he had merely been manipulating her in order to get his hands on her land.

Too late, a voice in her head mocked her.

Karen sighed. It was true—for better or for worse, she was already involved with the man who slept across the hall. No matter the reason, whether she lost him now or years from now, it would hurt.

By the time the first pale slivers of dawn crept into the sky, she was no more certain of what she needed to do than she had been when she'd crawled into her own bed the night before. Nor was she prepared for a face-to-face encounter with Grady so soon.

She crept downstairs, drank a quick cup of coffee and nibbled at a piece of toast, then all but ran to the barn and saddled her horse.

It was only a little past daybreak when she rode out on Ginger. The air was crisp and smelled of approaching snow. Thick gray clouds rolled across the sky. Karen rode hard for an hour, exhausting herself, the wind whipping at her hair and stinging her cheeks.

The exercise cleared her head, but as she rode back into the paddock, all of the turmoil came back with a vengeance at the sight of Grady waiting, a fierce scowl on his face.

"Where have you been?" he demanded, even as he helped her out of the saddle.

She shrugged off his hands. "I should think that would be obvious," she said, leading her horse into the heated barn to be unsaddled and rubbed down.

"Not to me, it isn't," he snapped. "I thought we had agreed you weren't going anywhere alone until we know what the hell is happening around here."

She flinched at the worry underscoring his words. She had completely forgotten about the danger in her haste to retreat from a different kind of threat.

"I'm sorry if you were worried," she said, meeting his gaze for the first time.

He sighed and raked his hand through his hair as he surveyed her from head to toe. "You didn't run into any problems?"

"None," she assured him. "I didn't see a single soul, nor was there any evidence of more fence down, sick cattle or anything else out of the ordinary."

Some of the concern faded from his eyes then, only to be replaced by what looked surprisingly like sorrow. "Why did you run?"

She thought about that, debated how truthful to be, then settled for total honesty. "I was afraid to see you because I knew I had hurt you last night."

He shrugged. "Yeah, well, I'll get over it."

"You shouldn't have to. What I did was unfair. I went to bed with you willingly. No, it was more than that," she corrected. "I went eagerly."

"And then you regretted it," he concluded.

"But not for the reason you think, not entirely anyway."

"You're going to have to explain that one to me."

It was hard to tell him, but she knew she owed him the truth. "The reason I felt lousy was because I felt so much more with you than I ever had with Caleb." When Grady would have spoken, she held up her hand. "I'm not comparing exactly. What Caleb and I had together was wonderful—our life, our marriage, all of it. I will never forget those feelings for as long as I live."

"How reassuring," Grady said with an unmistakable edge of bitterness.

Karen saw that she was going about this all wrong, but she was still sorting through her emotions herself. How could she be expected to explain them so Grady would understand? She knew, looking into his shadowed eyes, though, that she had to try, or they would be lost before they'd even begun. He had too much pride to stay with a woman whose heart would always belong to someone else.

"You like steak, right?" she asked.

He was clearly startled by the question. "You're going to get into a discussion of beef with me?"

"Just hear me out," she pleaded. "I'm trying to say this so you'll understand. Do you like steak?"

"I'm a cattle rancher. What do you think?"

"Okay, then—are all cuts of beef the same?"

"Of course not."

"So, they're the same, but different?" she prodded.

"Yes," he agreed, though he still looked puzzled by the analogy.

"A plain old strip steak is tasty, right? Enjoyable?" He nodded.

"But a filet takes it to a different level, wouldn't you agree?"

Understanding flared in his eyes, followed quickly by a hint of pure arrogance. "Are you saying I'm filet?"

She bit back a smile at the typically male response. "In a manner of speaking, but I wouldn't gloat about it if I were you," she warned. "I'm still not all that sure I'm ready for a steady diet of filet."

He grinned for the first time all morning. "I'll bet I can change your mind."

She regarded him with a mixture of amusement and impatience. "Men," she muttered. "Give them a compliment and it goes straight to their heads."

"Or other parts of their anatomy," Grady said, taking a step in her direction, then another, until he had her backed against a stall door.

When his mouth slanted across hers, her pulse leaped and her doubts fled. The kiss was persuasive, needy, maybe just a little desperate. But then, she was feeling a little desperate herself.

Feeling her senses swim, she was somehow reassured that last night's reaction hadn't been a fluke. Passion seethed just beneath the surface once again, ready to claim her and him.

Just not here and not now, she thought with a resigned sigh as Grady moved away, clearly satisfied by having made his point—that he could make her crave filet...crave him...any time he wanted.

That knowledge filled her with hope, and guilt, all over again. But the guilt wasn't as sharp somehow, she realized with a sense of bemusement. And that was something she would have to wrestle with another time.

Grady needed to get away. He'd claimed a victory of sorts with Karen in the barn. He'd gotten an admission from her that she wanted him just as badly now as she had the night before, even if she had a few demons left to fight.

But the temptation to haul her back upstairs was a little too powerful. That wasn't the answer for either of them. A little time and space were called for.

He sent her in to fix them both the breakfast they'd missed earlier, then went in search of Dooley to make sure he and Hank would be around to keep an eye on things. Assured that they wouldn't let Karen out of their sight, he joined her in the kitchen.

Over bacon and eggs, he announced his intention of going back to his place to make sure his foreman had everything under control and to pick up the things he'd need for the next few days.

"Now who's running scared?" she taunted.

"Maybe I am," he agreed, then offered, "You could always come along."

He watched her as she considered the challenge, then shook her head.

"No, I have things to do around here."

He regarded her intently, then warned, "If you leave the house, make sure Dooley or Hank knows where you are. Preferably take one of them with you."

She nodded.

Grady paused by her chair and pressed a kiss against her cheek. "We're going to work this out, darlin'. All of it."

"I know," she said softly, but with more conviction than she'd ever expressed before.

Once Grady was on the road, he found that the solitude he'd wanted wasn't nearly as comforting as he'd anticipated or hoped for. Increasingly impatient, he floored the accelerator and made it to his ranch in record time. Too restless to deal with the packing he'd intended to do, he went to the stables and saddled the fastest, most temperamental horse he owned. He needed a hard ride and a challenge. He didn't miss the irony of knowing that Karen had crept out of the house that morning, feeling the exact same desire.

At the top of a rise, he dismounted and surveyed the rugged terrain spread before him. It was enough. In fact, it was more than enough for him, for a legacy.

Getting the rest had been about pride, not need. He'd accepted the mission because it had been important to people he loved, to ancestors he'd wanted to honor. But maybe it wasn't his fight. Maybe it was time to let it go and seize what mattered most to him—Karen's love and the future they could have together.

Before he could be certain of that, he needed to see his grandfather one more time.

As if the old man had read his mind, he was waiting for Grady when he walked into the house after his ride. Glad as he was to see him, Grady was suspicious about the timing.

"What do you want?" Grady asked, regarding him cautiously.

"Is that any way to greet your own grandfather?"

"It is when this is the second visit you've paid recently, after years of insisting that I come to you."

"Well, my messages didn't seem to be getting any response. I came to see why."

"What messages?"

"The ones I've been leaving on that infernal machine of yours for days now."

"I must have missed them. I just got in. Is there a problem of some sort?"

"Why don't you tell me? I've been waiting for you since dawn. Either you went out very early or you never came home last night. I thought I heard your truck earlier, but you didn't come inside. Have you been with the lovely widow Hanson?"

Grady scowled. "Why do you insist on calling her that?"

"To remind you of who she is."

"Believe me, I grapple with that every minute of every day."

His grandfather's gaze narrowed. "But something's changed, hasn't it? You've finally realized that you're falling in love with her.''

"Perhaps," Grady agreed.

"And how does she feel about that?"

"She's struggling a bit with it."

"Yes, I imagine she would be. Her loyalty to her husband's memory is to be admired."

"It's damned inconvenient," Grady retorted, then sighed. "And admirable. Now let's get back to my original question. Why are you here?"

"I've been worried about you. I was afraid you might not recognize what was in front of your face until it was too late." He smiled, his expression satisfied. "I was wrong, so I'll be going."

"You want me to choose Karen over the land, don't you?" Grady said with some surprise. "That's what these unexpected little visits have been about."

"Getting the land always meant more to you than it did to me. And, yes, I think love is always more important than anything else. Your father knew that, even if he was unwise."

"You knew about him and Caleb's mother?" Grady asked, surprised by that.

"Only after the fact."

"How would you have counseled *him*—since you believe so strongly in love?"

For the first time in Grady's memory, his grandfather appeared at a loss. "Weighing love against a father's duty to a child is not a choice I would want to make. It turned out that everyone lost. That's the real tragedy."

He reached for Grady and gave him a fierce hug. "But you...you make me proud."

Grady's heart filled, his eyes stung. He had always

hoped to hear those words, always believed that the way to earn them was by reclaiming the land that had been stolen so long ago. But Thomas Blackhawk had surprised many people in his lifetime. Now Grady was among them.

"Thank you," he said, his voice husky with emotion.

"Just be happy."

Grady nodded. "I'm beginning to believe in happiness, Grandfather."

"And in love?"

"That, too." He just prayed that Karen would find her way to the same conclusion.

"How could I do it?" Karen asked, feeling miserable.

Uncomfortable with her own thoughts, she had called the Calamity Janes to come to her rescue. Those of her friends who were available had been at the ranch within the hour. To Karen's surprise, Lauren had arrived with Gina, claiming that she had a day off from shooting her latest movie and had wanted to check up on everyone back home. Only Cassie was missing, though she'd promised to drop by the second her shift ended at Stella's.

Now they were all seated around the kitchen table, cups of coffee in front of them, along with warm slices of a coffee cake Gina had whipped up within minutes of walking in the door. It was just like old times, though back then it had been brownies and chocolate chip cookies coming from the oven.

"How could you make love with a man as gorgeous as Grady?" Emma asked, forcing her to spell out what had her in such an emotional tizzy.

"How could I betray my husband is what I meant," Karen responded, changing the spin but not the reality.

"Caleb is dead," Gina reminded her gently. "And he wouldn't want you to be alone."

"Maybe not," she agreed. "But he wouldn't want me with Grady, not in a million years."

"Sorry, sweetie, but the choice isn't his to make," Emma said. "It's yours. Are you in love with him?"

Karen nodded. If she could tell the truth to anyone, it was these women who'd stood by her for years now. "I didn't want to be. I shouldn't be, but I am. There's no point in denying it anymore."

"Is he in love with you?" Gina asked.

"How can I know that? This all started over the land. How can I possibly trust him?"

"Sell me the land," Lauren said, repeating the offer she had made weeks ago. She scowled impatiently at the others. "Don't look at me like that. I'm serious. Being back here has reminded me of who I really am. Why do you think I keep turning up? I want to come home for good."

Karen considered what her friend was offering. Despite Lauren's insistence, Karen didn't believe for a minute that Lauren really wanted to own a ranch...but Grady didn't have to know that. She could tell him she planned to sell, see how he reacted. It would be the ultimate test of his feelings for her. She would finally know which mattered more to him—the land or their relationship.

"What's going on in that head of yours?" Gina asked, regarding her worriedly.

"I was just thinking about Lauren's offer."

Lauren's expression brightened. "Are you going to take me up on it?" she asked.

She sounded so eager that for a minute Karen almost believed that's what her friend really wanted.

"You could finally travel the globe, do all those things you dreamed about doing back in high school. And you'd have a place here any time you wanted it," Lauren added.

In her enthusiasm, Lauren didn't seem to be aware of the shocked gazes of the others, Karen included.

"Okay, Lauren, what's going on?" Emma demanded. "Why are you really pushing so hard for this? It doesn't have anything to do with helping Karen out, does it?"

"Of course it does," Lauren said indignantly.

"And?" Gina prodded. "What else? Why are you so anxious to flee Hollywood? What are you running away from? Is there another broken romance you haven't told us about?"

"I'm not fleeing anything. And I haven't been involved with anybody since my last divorce. I'm just thinking of embracing a different lifestyle."

"Why?" Gina repeated.

"Why not?" Lauren said with a shrug. Because she was such a good actress, she even managed to carry off the air of nonchalance, but none of them were buying it now.

Emma, who knew her best, finally sighed. "I guess we'll hear the real story when she wants us to know. We might as well stop badgering her."

"Good idea," Lauren said approvingly. She turned her attention back to Karen. "So? What have you decided? I've got my checkbook with me."

"I'm not going to sell the ranch to anybody,"

Karen said, feeling guilty at the disappointment that spread across Lauren's face. "I'm just going to let Grady think I might."

"You're testing him?" Gina asked, looking uneasy. "Do you think that's wise?"

"That could be the only way she ever finds out for sure what he really feels for her," Emma said, her expression thoughtful. She hesitated, then said slowly, "I say go for it."

"If he asks me, I'll back you up," Lauren agreed.

Karen turned to Gina. "Well?"

Gina sighed. "Do what you have to do," she said with obvious reluctance. "But lying has a way of backfiring. If it were me, I'd take a different route, but then I've had a lot of bad experiences with liars lately."

"Care to explain that?" Emma asked.

"Nope," Gina said. "Let's get one life straightened out at a time. Mine can wait."

After making that ominous declaration, Gina excused herself and departed, leaving the rest of them staring silently after her.

"It has something to do with that mysterious man who's been hanging around," Lauren said. "I know it does."

"Pestering her for answers won't do a bit of good. When it comes to being tight-lipped, Gina's even worse than Lauren," Emma said, grinning across the table at the woman she'd just accused of keeping too many secrets.

"Spend a little time having your life splashed across the front pages of the tabloids and you'll keep your own counsel, too," Lauren retorted. "Come on, Emma, my ride just abandoned me. Take me back

into town. I think we ought to be long gone before
the sexy Mr. Blackhawk returns. He might come to
the conclusion we've been out here conspiring against
him, especially when he hears what Karen has to say
about selling the ranch to me. I don't want to be
around when he concludes I've stabbed him in the
back. He doesn't seem like the kind of man to take
defeat really well.''

Karen hugged her friends goodbye, straightened up
the kitchen and put a roast in the oven for dinner. She
might as well feed Grady well before she broke the
bad—albeit false—news to him.

It seemed to Karen there was something different
about Grady when he got back to the ranch shortly
before supper time. He looked relaxed, more at peace
in some way she couldn't quite define. The kiss he
brushed across her lips was lighthearted, as was his
teasing "Hi, honey, I'm home.''

She regarded him intently. ''You certainly seem to
be in a good mood.''

''I am,'' he said.

And she was about to ruin it, she thought despondently. Oh, well, it had to be done.

But maybe not until after dinner.

''Put your things away. Dinner will be ready in
about fifteen minutes.''

''Smells delicious. What are we having?''

''Roast beef.''

He grinned. ''Not filet?''

She chuckled at the taunt. ''That remains to be
seen.''

All during dinner she struggled with herself, trying
to force the lie about an impending sale past her lips,

but the mood was too special, too sensual, too emotionally charged, to deliberately ruin it. At least that's what she told herself when she stayed silent right on through dessert and afterward, when she found herself once more in Grady's arms.

"Make love with me," he whispered as he held her.

Karen gazed into his eyes, saw the heat and longing there, and couldn't resist.

His touches were magic, just as they had been before. Her body pulsed and throbbed and burned with each increasingly intimate caress.

And when he entered her, she felt that same astonishing sense of fulfillment even as her senses spun out of control.

In the peaceful aftermath, Grady held her. Tonight there were no tears to spoil the closeness, just the dread of a lie she was determined to tell.

Finally, when their breathing had eased and their bodies had cooled, she dared to broach the subject of the ranch.

"I had an offer on the ranch today." That much at least was true, which made the words easier to get out. Yet guilt flowed through her when she felt his body go still.

"Oh?"

"Lauren's interested."

Grady didn't seem nearly as shocked by that as she might have expected. Or maybe it was just that he was totally focused on what the news meant for him and his determination to restore the land of his ancestors to Blackhawk control.

"Have you accepted?" he asked, his voice neutral.

"I'm considering it."

"I see. Mind telling me why you'll consider her offer and not mine?"

Karen hesitated. This was tricky territory, even trickier than the blatant lie she had just told. He deserved honesty, though, at least about this.

"You know why," she said.

"Because of Caleb. Even though you know that his animosity toward me wasn't justified."

She nodded.

Grady met her gaze, his expression sad but accepting. "I think what you and I have found these past few months is something special, but he's always going to be between us, isn't he?"

"No," she said. "Not Caleb. The land. I'm afraid to trust what you and I have because of the land. I know how badly you want it, and if it were mine alone to give, it would be yours. But it's mine only because my husband died trying to protect it. I have to consider his feelings."

For a moment he seemed to be struggling with himself over something, but then his expression hardened.

"So sell it," he said bitterly. "Get it out from between us. Then we'll see where we go from there."

She didn't know how to interpret his expression or his words. She did know that when he left the bed and the house, her heart went with him.

Chapter Fourteen

Grady had struggled to keep a lid on his temper when Karen had made her big announcement about possibly selling the ranch to Lauren. He'd seen straight through the ploy. Maybe Lauren had made an offer on the land, maybe she hadn't, but Karen had been deliberately testing him. Looking back on the exchange, he pretty sure he hadn't passed it with flying colors.

Oh, he'd told her to sell it, but he'd said it grudgingly, no doubt about it. He'd set up a test of his own—sell and then we'll see if there's anything between us. They were quite a pair. Despite everything they'd shared, trust was severely lacking. He wondered if they'd ever have any faith in each other's motives…in each other's love.

Why hadn't he simply countered with an announcement of his own? Why hadn't he told her of the conclusion he'd reached earlier in the day, that she mattered more to him than the ranch?

That one was easy. Because, despite knowing that a relationship with her was more important, it had hurt that she was deliberately trying to back him into a corner, to rob him of something she knew he had valid reasons for wanting.

He rode hard over his own acres for the next few days, trying to push Karen out of his head, but she wouldn't go. He made almost hourly calls to Dooley and Hank to make sure that she was safe, that there had been no new incidents. He'd been careful to skirt the real reason for his absence, letting them conclude that he'd had sudden business to attend to at his own ranch. Dooley grumbled that they weren't getting a lick of work done with all the baby-sitting they were doing.

"I suggest you not describe sticking close to Karen as baby-sitting," he suggested wryly. "I doubt she'd appreciate it."

"Nope," Dooley agreed, not sounding the least bit remorseful. "And to tell the truth, she's getting tired of seeing our faces around all the time. When are you coming back over here?"

"I'm not sure," Grady said honestly.

"Well, hurry it up. Hank and me have real work to do now that the weather's beginning to turn for the better."

"I'll try to wrap things up over here soon," Grady promised. Just as soon as he finished kicking himself in the butt for walking out on Karen in the first place.

At the end of the week, when he turned up alone at Stella's, craving company as much as food, Grady

weathered the stormy expression in Cassie's eyes
when he slid into a booth at the back.

"Why aren't you at the ranch with Karen?" she
demanded. Evidently she was unaware of the fact that
he'd been gone for days now. She regarded him with
an accusing look. "When she refused to stay with
Cole and me, you promised to keep an eye on her."

"Hank and Dooley have everything out there under
control," he assured her. "I checked with them less
than twenty minutes ago."

"I hope you're right," she said direly. "Because
if anything happens to her, Grady Blackhawk, you'll
have all of us to answer to."

Grady took the threat seriously, but it was no match
for the guilt he would live with for the rest of his life
if something went wrong because of his own stupid
pride. He sighed. It was time to face the music.

"Make that meat loaf to go," he said, sliding back
out of the booth.

"I hope it wasn't something I said," Cassie told
him with total insincerity.

He frowned at her. "You know damn well it was.
In fact, double the order. I might as well take a peace
offering with me."

She grinned. "Take the roast chicken instead. It's
her favorite."

"Whatever you say."

He packed the two dinners into the truck and
headed toward Karen's, anticipation mounting with
each mile he covered. He envisioned a little fussing
and feuding when she first spotted him, but he ought
to be able to get around that with an abject apology.
Hell, he'd even help her draw up the papers to sell

the ranch to Lauren, if that was what she really wanted.

And once Karen had accepted the sincerity of his apology, they could make up the way men and women had been getting back on track for years—in bed. The prospect had him stepping down just a little harder on the accelerator.

Grady was less than a mile away from the ranch when he thought he smelled smoke. As he rounded the last curve in the road, he spotted an orange glow on the horizon that had nothing to do with the setting sun. Panic crawled up his throat and made it impossible to swallow.

Sweet heaven, he thought, just as a car made a squealing turn out of the driveway onto the highway, nearly sideswiping the truck, before speeding past him in a blur. Shock had him hitting his brakes and staring, first in one direction, then the other.

There was no question about it, the ranch was on fire.

And the person most likely responsible had just come within inches of running him off the road.

Karen had just gotten out of the shower and pulled on her old flannel pajamas when she thought she smelled smoke. No sooner had the thought registered than the smoke detectors downstairs went off in a simultaneous blast of sound.

She jammed her feet into a pair of shoes, grabbed her robe and raced for the stairs. Thick gray smoke was already swirling at the foot of the steps.

''Think,'' she ordered herself. ''Take just a second and think.''

There was a rope ladder by the bedroom window.

She could get out that way. It was safer than risking running straight into the fire the second she reached the first floor. And judging from the number of alarms blaring at once, the fire was already too widespread for her to be able to put it out herself, assuming she could even get to the fire extinguisher she kept in the kitchen.

Turning back to the bedroom, she paused long enough to grab the cordless phone and dial nine-one-one.

"It's already bad," she told the emergency operator. "I can't see the flames, but the smoke is all through the downstairs."

"Can you get out?" Birdie Cox asked, her manner calm and reassuring, even as she was barking directions to the ranch into a speaker that would rouse all the volunteer firefighters in the area. "Are you on a portable phone, hon?"

"Yes and I'm going out the bedroom window," Karen said. "I have a rope ladder. I'll be fine."

"Look below," Birdie advised. "Make sure there are no flames coming out of the windows downstairs. Now you leave this line open, tuck the phone in your pocket and go. I want you to tell me when you're safely on the ground, you hear me?"

"You'll be the first to know," Karen promised as she dropped the ladder out the window after first looking to make sure it was safe. Smoke was billowing out, but there were no flames.

Taking a deep breath, she forced herself to climb through the window and onto the ladder. It wasn't a long drop, but she didn't look down again until she felt the ground under her feet. Then she stepped back and took a good, long look at the house, trying to assess where the worst of the fire was located.

"Birdie, I'm outside and I'm okay," she reported. "It looks to me like the worst of this is in the front of the house."

"I've got two fire engines and a dozen men on the way. Don't try to be a heroine. Sit tight and let them handle this."

Even as Birdie spoke, Karen could hear the distant wail of a siren and something else—the frantic shouting of her name.

"Dammit, Karen, where are you?"

Dear God, it sounded as if it was coming from inside the house, and there was no mistaking the fact that it was Grady. She raced toward the front door, screaming as she ran.

"Grady, I'm outside. Grady!"

She was halfway up the front steps when she spotted him silhouetted in the thick smoke. He turned slowly, then bent over, coughing. Frantic, she almost ran toward him, but he began moving again, dodging flames and falling debris.

He was still coughing when he reached her, and there were streaks of ash on his face and holes made by burning cinders on his clothes, but she'd never been so glad to see anyone in her life. She threw herself into his arms. They tightened around her at once, and she could feel a shudder course through him.

"Thank God," he murmured. "I saw the flames just as I turned in." He held her away from him. "Are you okay? Were you inside? What happened?"

The rush of adrenaline that had kept her on her feet

suddenly evaporated, and her knees went weak. She sagged against him.

"Oh, darlin'," he whispered, holding her. "It's okay."

Feeling safe at last, she finally dared to look at the house, where flames were roaring through the roof even as volunteer firefighters began swarming everywhere. Tears stung her eyes and spilled down her cheeks. All of her memories were in that house and they were being completely destroyed in that terrible inferno. It was as if her life were going up in flames. How could anything ever be okay again?

The streams of water being directed at the house merely sizzled and steamed in the heat, doing little to dampen the blaze.

When she moaned at the sight, Grady scooped Karen up and carried her to his truck, tucked her inside, then turned on the heater. He found a blanket in back to wrap her in, then climbed in behind the wheel.

His fingers slid into her hair, and he caressed her cheek with the pad of his thumb. "Talk to me, Karen. Are you okay? You're not hurt, are you? Did you get burned?"

"No," she whispered, her voice choked. "What happened? How did this happen?"

Grady's expression turned grim. "Maybe we ought to wait and see what the firemen have to say about that. And Michael should be here soon. I called him."

She regarded him suspiciously. "Why did you call the sheriff? You think this was deliberately set, don't you?" she said, without waiting for his reply.

"Don't *you?*" he asked mildly. "Or did you leave the stove on? Or maybe forget to put the screen in front of the fireplace? Or was there a short in some wiring?''

She frowned at his mocking tone. ''It could have been any of those things,'' she said, not ready to believe the alternative—that someone had deliberately burned down her home.

''Really?'' he asked with blatant skepticism.

''Okay, no, I hadn't turned the stove on all evening. And there was no fire in the fireplace. But it could have been the wiring,'' she insisted stubbornly. ''It's old.''

''Whatever,'' he said. ''Where are Hank and Dooley?''

''I haven't seen them since before supper time,'' she said. ''I told them to take the night off.''

He stared at her incredulously. ''Why did you do *that?*''

''Because they'd been watching me nonstop for days now. They needed a break.''

''Sit here,'' Grady ordered, looking more furious than she'd ever seen him.

She was shivering too badly not to comply. Even with the heater blasting and a blanket wrapped around her, she was cold. An aftereffect of the shock, she supposed.

''Where are you going?''

''To check the bunkhouse, then to take a look around. Maybe they've pitched in to help the firefighters.''

She nodded and watched him go. Only as he walked away did she wonder at the coincidence of Grady arriving for the first time in days just as a fire destroyed the ranch that stood between them.

* * *

Grady was furious enough to knock some heads together. Dooley should have known better than to leave. Hadn't they talked about this a dozen times a day? Karen was never to be left alone, not even if she insisted.

When he reached the bunkhouse, there was no sign of either man. Of course, if they'd been on the property in the first place they would have heard the sirens, if not smelled the smoke, and run to help. Which meant they'd left, probably for a night on the town.

On his way back to the truck, he kept an eye out for either of the hands, but he was within sight of Karen when he spotted the two men climbing from Hank's pickup, horror evident in their expressions as they stared at the charred, smoldering ruins of Karen's home.

"What the hell happened?" Dooley asked when he spotted Grady.

"That's what I intended to ask you. Why were the two of you away from here tonight?"

"The boss insisted," Hank said defensively.

"I told you we shouldn't listen," Dooley grumbled. "We should have stayed right here, just the way Grady told us to."

"Where'd you go?" Grady asked.

"Into town."

"Winding River?"

"No, the other direction, over to Little Creek. There's a bar over there with country music on the juke box and some pretty waitresses. It's usually packed with hands from all over," Hank said. "We didn't stay long. We had supper and came straight back, because Dooley here was nagging me like an old woman.'' Hank's gaze strayed back to the fire. ''Guess he was right to be worried.''

Grady paused, thinking about that. ''See anyone you recognized?''

''The place was packed. It's Saturday night, pay-day for most of the men around here,'' Dooley said.

''Think,'' Grady said. ''Was there anybody in there you knew?''

For a long time neither man responded. Then Dooley glanced at Hank. ''Didn't I see you talking to Joe Keeley?''

''Who's that?'' Grady asked.

''He works for the Oldhams,'' Hank said.

So, Grady thought, the Oldhams could have known that Karen was here at the ranch unprotected. One glance at Dooley and he saw that the old man had reached the same conclusion.

''You thinking what I'm thinking?'' Dooley asked.

''We should tell the sheriff and let him deal with this,'' Grady said, though he was itching to take on the task himself. The image of Karen's tear-filled eyes and heartbroken expression was the deciding factor.

''Let's go,'' he said grimly. He faced Hank. ''Karen's in my truck. You go over there and sit with her. This time I don't care if she tries to bribe you with a million bucks, you don't let her out of your sight until we're back. Is that clear?''

Hank nodded. ''I'm sorry about what happened,'' he said, casting a devastated look toward the house. ''It's been so peaceful around here lately, I thought it would be okay.''

''I know,'' Grady said.

''If she asks where you've gone, what do I tell her?'' Hank asked.

Grady smiled ruefully. "I suppose telling her not to worry her pretty little head about it is a bad idea."

"Real bad," Dooley concurred. "At least if you expect her to be talking to you again."

Grady nodded. "Then tell her we've gone to visit a neighbor and that we hope to come back with some answers about what happened tonight."

"That's going to bring her running right after us," Dooley pointed out.

"Not if Hank does his job," Grady said grimly.

"Yeah, well, sometimes the boss has a way of sneaking around the best intentions," Dooley said.

Grady exchanged a look with Hank. Satisfied, he said, "Not this time."

He was counting on her staying put, just where he'd left her. Later they could argue about how macho and chauvinistic his behavior was. In fact, he'd be happy to discuss it with her for hours on end, once they were both safely tucked in his bed.

"He went *where?*" Karen's shout echoed in the cab of Grady's truck. It had gotten too hot some time ago, so she'd turned off the engine. The temperature had climbed another ten degrees just since Hank had made his announcement about Grady taking off to do a little informal investigating.

Hank winced under her accusing scowl. "To see a neighbor."

"Without discussing it with me," she muttered, mostly to herself.

"He was in kind of a hurry," Hank said, defending Grady's sneaky departure. "Dooley's with him. He'll be okay."

"I'm not worried about his safety. In fact, I'm considering strangling him myself. Didn't he think for one single second that I might have a right to be in on this little visit?''

"Actually that did come up," Hank said. "He thought you'd be better off here."

Fury had her seeing red. "Oh, he did, did he?"

"I think he knew you might not like that," Hank said, clearly trying to help by pointing out Grady's deep understanding of her psyche.

"But he didn't stop for one minute to reconsider, did he?" she snapped.

"No, ma'am."

"Okay, then," she murmured. She would just have to take matters into her own hands. "Hank, start the truck."

"Ma'am?" He looked as if he'd rather climb on the back of a horse straight out of the wild.

"Which part of 'start the truck' did you not understand?" She reached for the key and gave it a twist. The truck sputtered, but didn't start. "Get the picture?"

"Yes, ma'am, but I think it's a really bad idea."

She frowned at him. "Why is that?"

"Because Grady's counting on you staying right here."

"I'm sure he'll learn to live with his mistake," she snapped. "Start the car, Hank, or get out of my way."

With painfully obvious reluctance, Hank started the truck, then put it in gear. "Where are we going?"

She frowned at the question. Hank had been very careful not to indicate which neighbor Grady suspected of involvement in the fire. She was reasonably certain he didn't intend to share that piece of information now, which explained the deliberately vague expression on his face.

"If you don't take me wherever those two men have gone, I swear to you I will not only fire you, but I will destroy any chance of your getting a job on any other ranch in Wyoming. Hell, I'll make sure you don't work anywhere in the whole damned country."

Hank regarded her with an injured look. "I'm just trying to do my job, ma'am, the way Grady told me to."

"You don't work for Grady," she reminded him, clinging to her patience by a thread.

"Maybe not, but the last time I ignored one of his orders, look what happened." He stared miserably toward the smoldering remains of the house.

Karen sighed. "Turn off the engine."

Hank nodded, looking relieved. "Good decision, ma'am." His expression brightened. "And just in the nick of time, too. Here comes the sheriff."

Karen glanced outside and saw Michael approaching the truck, his step weary.

"You okay?" he asked, when she stepped outside to greet him, still swaddled in the blanket.

"I've been better," she said honestly. She nodded toward the house. "What's the verdict?"

"Arson," he said succinctly. "Not much doubt about it. There was evidence of gasoline about thirty yards from the living room window, along with some scraps of rags. Whoever did this probably tossed a firebomb into the house. I'm surprised you didn't hear glass breaking."

"I was taking a shower when it started."

"Lucky for you you were upstairs. It gave you time to get out before the fire spread. Looks as if it moved pretty quick through the downstairs.'' He glanced into the truck and spotted Hank. It seemed to take him by surprise. "I thought Grady was with you.''

"He was here until a little while ago.''

"Where is he now?''

"He and Dooley are checking into something," she said evasively.

"You sure about that?''

"Of course," she said, ignoring that brief flicker of doubt she'd felt earlier. This was no time to be discussing coincidences with the sheriff.

"You don't think maybe he got nervous watching me poke around out here?'' Michael asked.

"He's the one who called you," she reminded him.

Michael nodded, though he didn't look completely satisfied. "So he did. Where did he go to do this checking?''

"I'm not sure," she said truthfully.

"Well, I'm going over to have another word with the fire chief.'' His somber gaze locked with hers. "I'd suggest you track down your friend and get him back here, because if I have to go hunting for him, he's going to pop right back to the top of my list of suspects.''

She watched as Michael walked away, then turned back to Hank. "You heard?''

He nodded.

"We have to warn him, Hank.''

The young hand sighed heavily and started the truck. "Let's go.''

Karen climbed back in and patted his knee. "Don't worry. You're doing the right thing.''

"If you say so.''

"I do. It'll be so much better if I wring his neck, instead of waiting for the sheriff to do it.''

Chapter Fifteen

The minute Grady saw Jesse Oldham's car parked behind his barn, instinct told him that it was the same car he'd spotted earlier leaving Karen's. Even though it was cold enough to cool an engine quickly, he touched the hood. Was there a lingering trace of heat? Or was that merely wishful thinking after all this time?

"What do you think?" Dooley asked.

"Nothing yet. I'm keeping an open mind," Grady insisted as he opened the unlocked car and sniffed the air. This time he knew it wasn't his imagination playing tricks when he caught a whiff of gasoline. Just in case, he called Dooley closer, then stepped aside. "Lean in there. What do you smell?"

"Gasoline, plain as day," Dooley said, his blue eyes snapping with indignation. "I'm gonna murder that man with my bare hands."

"Not without my help," Grady said grimly.

They stalked across the yard. When Dooley would have politely knocked on the fancy oak door, Grady shouldered it open, shouting for Jesse as he entered the dimly lit foyer.

"What the hell's the ruckus?" Jesse demanded sleepily, all but stumbling from a room on the left where the flickering of pale light suggested he'd been comfortably watching TV. For just an instant, alarm flared in his eyes when he spotted Grady.

"What are you doing here?" he asked.

"Can't a neighbor pay a friendly visit?" Grady asked.

"You just about broke my front door down. What's friendly about that? Besides, you're not my neighbor. If there's any justice in this world, you never will be."

Grady regarded him silently for a full minute, watching his nervousness increase. "Oh?" he said finally. "Why is that? Surely you don't think I care whether there's a burned out house on the land I've had my eye on."

Just as Grady had expected, Jesse didn't show so much as a hint of surprise at the announcement. "You don't seem shocked," Grady noted.

"About the fire?" Jesse said with a shrug. "Why would I be? The police scanner's been blaring the news for the past couple of hours now. Never heard such a commotion."

That was one explanation, Grady thought, impressed by the man's quick thinking. "I imagine it has," he agreed. "But I'm thinking there might be another reason you know all about Karen losing her home tonight."

Jesse regarded him defiantly. "Such as?"

"Being there when it started," Grady suggested. "That was you who almost ran me off the road tonight, wasn't it?"

Jesse's expression faltered just a bit at the accusation. "I wasn't anywhere near the place. I've been in there right smack in front of the TV all night long."

"And your wife can vouch for that?"

"She went to bed early. Had one of her migraines. Started round about supper time."

"What about Kenny?" Dooley asked. "Where's he been tonight?"

"I don't keep track of my son's comings and goings. He's a teenager. They roam all over the place. I know for certain that he's in his room right now. Heard him come in."

"When was that?" Grady asked. If Kenny Oldham had returned at any time in the past two hours, that would leave him wide-open as a suspect. Jesse seemed to be struggling to do the math.

"Beats me," he said at last. "I fell asleep." His smile suggested he was proud of his ingenuity.

"Really? Yet you heard all about the fire on your scanner?"

Jesse nodded, that smile fading into feigned sympathy. "Felt real bad about it, too."

"But not bad enough to get your son and go over there to help out. You are a volunteer firefighter, aren't you?" Grady guessed, knowing that most of the men around here were. At the very least, they pitched in to help save a neighbor's property when a tragedy like this struck.

"Nope," Jesse said, tapping his chest. "Bad ticker. Used to help out, but no more."

Grady was about to demand that Jesse call his son down to be questioned, when the front door burst open again and Karen came in, trailed by an apologetic-looking Hank.

"Sorry," Hank said. "There's a real good reason we're here."

Grady scowled at the pair of them, but his gaze rested longest on Karen. There were dark smudges under her too-bright eyes and her complexion was still very pale.

"What might that be?" he asked.

Karen looked from him to Jesse and back again. Whatever had brought her running over here seemed to have been forgotten. She faced her longtime neighbor.

"Did you do it?" she asked bluntly.

Jesse returned her gaze uneasily. "Like I told your friends here, I haven't left the house all night."

"Unfortunately, he's not quite as capable of accounting for his son's whereabouts," Grady said.

Karen looked shocked. "Kenny? He used to sit in my kitchen and eat cookies while I visited with his mother. Surely he wouldn't set my house on fire."

"He would if he was real anxious to get his daddy's approval," Dooley said, speaking up for the first time since Grady's interrogation had begun in earnest. "That boy's always been crying out for some man to look at him like he's worth something. Jesse here's been too busy to give him the time of day, since he's not big enough or strong enough to play football, isn't that right, Jesse?"

Even as Dooley made the accusation, Grady thought he saw movement on the stairs. He glanced up and caught sight of Kenny, hovering on the land-ing. Given what Dooley had just said about the teen's relationship with his father, he felt a stirring of pity for him.

"Come on down here, son," Grady said.

Kenny crept down the stairs, his terrified gaze locked on his father. As Dooley had said, he was slight for sixteen, his body not yet filled out. At the foot of the steps, he instinctively edged closer to Karen. She reached out and took his hand, then gave it a squeeze.

"Kenny, did you start that fire?" she asked, her voice filled with hurt.

Tears welled up in the boy's eyes, but he nodded, his gaze never leaving her face. "I'm sorry," he whispered. "I didn't know it would be so bad. I swear I didn't. I just thought it would scare you, the way Daddy said. He said we had to have that land or we'd never be certain whether our herd would have water. Mama argued with him. She told him you would never cut us off, but he said you'd be selling out soon enough and the new owner might not be nearly so concerned with an old piece of paper drawn up between friends. It wasn't even notarized."

Even as she held the boy's hand, Karen scowled at his father. "You coward," she accused. "You didn't even have the guts to do the job yourself. You counted on Kenny's need to please you. What kind of father are you? You're not even a man. You're scum. And if you were worried about those water rights before, you'd better be on your knees praying now, because I'll see you in hell before I ever let your herd near that creek again, paper or no paper. I'll find some way to see that it's voided."

When she swayed on her feet, Grady stepped

closer, but she steadied herself, then took one last, scathing look at Jesse Oldham and turned to leave.

"Let's get out of here before I'm sick to my stomach," she said. She touched Kenny's tearstained cheek. "Thank you for having the courage to tell us what really happened tonight."

"Hank, how about sticking around here till we can get the sheriff over here?" Grady asked. "Somebody ought to keep an eye on things." He lowered his voice. "Make sure Oldham doesn't do anything to that boy, all right?"

"I'll stay with him," Dooley said. "He'll need a way home."

Grady nodded. "I'll call the sheriff. Then I'm taking Karen home with me." He glanced at her for a reaction, but her face was expressionless. He took that for agreement, or maybe she was simply too wiped out to object.

"We'll see you in the morning," he told the two men. "And Dooley, thanks for helping me out tonight. You be sure and tell the sheriff how helpful Kenny was."

"No problem. I just hope a court can distinguish between a mixed-up boy who set that fire and the man who put the notion into his head."

Grady nodded. "We'll see that they do."

He led Karen to the car and settled her inside, then felt his heart clutch at the despair on her face. He couldn't help feeling he'd set all of this into motion by making it so plain to one and all that he intended to buy her ranch. Maybe that was what had set off Jesse Oldham's paranoia about those water rights.

"I'm sorry," he said.

She glanced up, clearly startled. "Why? You didn't have anything to do with this."

"Jesse might not have tried anything if he'd thought his water rights were safe," he said.

She shook her head. "This started long before you came into the picture. He didn't trust Caleb to honor them either, remember?"

That was true enough, Grady supposed, but it didn't seem to lessen his own sense of guilt. He was silent for the entire drive to his ranch, though he couldn't help sneaking a glance at Karen from time to time. He'd never seen her looking quite so lost.

At his house, he led her inside, then pointed out the master bathroom. "Take a warm bath, why don't you? I'll call your friends and let them know what happened and that you'll be staying here for a bit. There's a robe on the back of the door. It'll be too big, but it'll keep you warm enough."

She nodded, then retreated into the bathroom and closed the door. Feeling unbearably tired, he stood there listening to the sound of water running. Only when it had cut off and he heard the subtle splash suggesting that she'd climbed into the deep tub did he go back to the kitchen and put a pan of milk on the stove. Maybe a cup of warm milk would help both of them get some sleep.

Then he called Cassie's house. He was relieved when Cole answered. He explained what had happened.

"We can be over there in an hour if she needs us," Cole said.

"I think she needs a good night's sleep more. Come in the morning, why don't you?"

"We'll be there," Cole promised. "Cassie and I will call the others."

"I'd appreciate it," Grady said, relieved not to have to go through the explanation of the night's events again and again.

"Grady?"

"Yes?"

"I'm glad you're there for her. She's going to need you."

"I'm not so sure about that," Grady said. "I can't help thinking that when she thinks it through, she'll blame me for setting it all into motion."

"No," Cole said. "She's going to blame herself for not protecting Caleb's legacy. It's up to all of us, you included, to make sure she understands how wrong that is, that this was out of her control."

With Cole's words still echoing in his head, Grady was less surprised when Karen walked into the kitchen, her face drawn, her eyes dull. She accepted a mug of warm milk, then sank wearily onto a chair.

"I've been thinking," she said dully. "I have to rebuild. It's what Caleb would want."

Grady wanted to shout that Caleb was dead, that his wishes no longer mattered, but he couldn't. She wasn't ready to hear that.

Instead, he simply asked, "What do you want?"

She blinked in surprise at the question. "To rebuild," she said a little too readily.

"Really?"

"Of course."

He started to point out that the ranch was draining the life out of her, just as it had from Caleb, but he kept silent. She wasn't ready to hear that, either. To his deep regret, he realized that maybe she never would be.

Karen spent the night wrapped in Grady's arms. He didn't make love to her, as if he understood that her emotions were too fragile right now to bear it. She loved him for understanding that much about her. In fact, she loved him for being beside her all during the long ordeal of the fire and its aftermath. The truth was, she would probably go on loving him forever.

Unfortunately, she couldn't tell him that, or be with him. She had a duty to Caleb to honor first. It seemed she might never be free of that terrible sense of obligation.

In the morning, when Cassie, Cole, Gina and Emma arrived together on Grady's doorstep, she was passed from embrace to embrace. She felt as limp as a rag doll, but she forced a smile to reassure them all that she was okay.

"Okay, then, what are your plans?" Emma asked briskly as they sat around the table, while Gina instinctively moved to the stove to whip up a hearty breakfast.

Grady looked at her across the table. "You can stay here for as long as you like," he said.

She was tempted. Oh, how she was tempted, but she shook her head. "There's another room in the bunkhouse. I'll move in there while the house is being rebuilt."

When everyone stared at her incredulously, she returned their gazes with a touch of defiance. "What?" she demanded.

"Why are you doing that?" Cassie demanded. "You know you don't want to."

"Of course, I do. Caleb—"

"Is dead," Cassie snapped, then cast a belligerent look at the others. "I'm sorry, but it's true and it's what the rest of you are thinking."

"Still, I owe it to him," Karen insisted. A glance at Grady made her sigh. He looked resigned. No, worse than that, he looked unbearably sad.

"I'm sorry," she added in a whisper meant for him alone.

He gave a curt nod. "I know."

No one seemed to know what to say after that. Gina's breakfast cooled on the plates in front of them, until she finally stood impatiently, gathered up the plates and scraped the leftovers into the trash.

"Leave the dishes," Grady said. "I'll do them later."

"Then I guess we should be on our way," Cole said, casting a sympathetic look at Grady and a worried one toward Karen.

"Can you give me a lift home?" Karen asked him.

"I'll take you home," Grady said tersely.

"But—"

"I'll take you," he repeated.

She nodded, then hugged the others. "Thanks for coming over."

"If you need anything, anything at all, call us," Emma said fiercely. "And I expect you in town later today to go shopping. You'll need some clothes."

Karen realized that hadn't even occurred to her. She didn't own so much as a toothbrush. Suddenly it was all too much for her. The last bit of stoic resolve collapsed. The tears she'd been battling since last night poured down her cheeks. Great, gulping sobs welled up deep inside.

It was Grady who gathered her in his arms. Grady who murmured soothing reassurances when the others reluctantly left. Karen cried until there were no tears left, until Grady's shirt was soaked and her face was swollen.

"Oh, God, I must look awful," she said with a hitch in her voice.

"You look beautiful," he said.

"Liar."

"Not about that," he insisted. "You will always be beautiful to me."

She lifted her gaze to his, saw his heart in his eyes. "I love you," she said. "But I have to do this. Please tell me that you understand."

"I don't," he said, wiping the tears from her cheeks. "Not really. But it doesn't matter. It's enough that you believe this is what you have to do."

"I don't know what will happen," she told him honestly. "I can't ask you to wait. In fact, you should probably give up on me."

He smiled at that. "Never." His caress lingered on her cheek. "When the house is built and you're ready to move on with your life, I'll be waiting."

The promise gave her strength. Maybe what she was about to do was sheer folly, but she knew that she wouldn't be free until she had done it. A new house, a thriving ranch, would be her gift to Caleb's memory. Maybe then she would finally be able to walk away and into the life with Grady that she so desperately wanted.

Grady was bombarded by information on the progress of the new ranch house. What Dooley and Hank didn't report, one of Karen's friends did. They kept him so completely in the loop that he knew the instant the paint had dried on the new kitchen walls. He knew within seconds when the last workman had left.

"Go over there," Cassie pleaded, not for the first time.

"No," he said flatly, regretting his impulse to have dinner at Stella's.

Cassie ignored his scowl and slid into the booth opposite him. "She loves you. I know she does."

"I know it, too," he agreed.

"Then why won't you go to see her?"

"She has to want what I'm offering bad enough to come to me."

"What exactly are you offering?" Cassie demanded.

"A future," he said.

"Does she know that?"

"Of course she does."

"Really? Did you propose to her? If so, I must have missed it."

He frowned again. "Not in so many words," he mumbled.

"What was that?"

"I said I didn't propose in so many words."

"Well, then, is it any wonder she hasn't come to you? You've ignored her for four months. She probably—no, make that definitely—assumes you've lost interest. Not that she'd ever blame you. Isn't that precisely what she told you to do, to forget about her?"

"She told you that?"

Cassie sighed. "No, she doesn't say much of anything. She just works day and night. She's going to keel over if somebody doesn't stop her."

"And you think I ought to be that somebody," he guessed.

"If you love her the way you claim to," she challenged. "None of the rest of us are getting through to her."

He scowled at her, but she didn't back down. "Okay, okay," he said, tossing his napkin on the table. "I'll go to see her."

"With an engagement ring," she called after him.

"No, something even more convincing," he retorted, and let the door of Stella's slam behind him before Cassie could demand details.

And before she realized that he'd just stuck her with his bill. He figured she owed him the meal, since she hadn't let him eat it in peace.

He rode out to the ranch, walked into the den and picked up the paper he'd had drawn up months ago, along with another packet that he'd been holding for the right time. For good measure, he also grabbed the little jewelry box that had been tucked into his desk drawer just as long. The latter would definitely have made Cassie happy if she'd known about it. He had a feeling, though, that it was the papers that were going to make the difference with Karen, if anything did.

He was about to leave when his grandfather stepped through the front door. He took one look at the papers and the box in Grady's hand and gave a nod of approval.

"About time," he said, heading for the living room and lowering himself heavily into a chair, groaning a bit with the effort. He was playing the role of aging family scion to the hilt.

"Make yourself at home, why don't you?" Grady said sarcastically.

"I intend to, and this time I'm not leaving until you've talked that woman into marrying you. I'd like to see one great-grandbaby before I die."

Grady grinned at him, impressed with the performance. Last he'd heard, the family doctor had said that Thomas Blackhawk would outlive them all.

"With any luck, we'll give you half a dozen," he promised. If this was what his grandfather really wanted from him, he was all too eager to grant the request.

"Not unless you get the woman to say yes," the old man said wryly.

"I will," Grady said with confidence. He'd been waiting too damned long to take anything less than a yes for an answer.

Karen was hanging laundry when she saw Grady's car leave the highway and tear up the driveway creating a swirl of dust. Her heart went still and her hands rested motionless on the clothesline. The late August sun burned her shoulders.

She watched warily as Grady came toward her, his gaze seeking hers, that incredible swagger making her blood run hot. It had been far too long since she'd seen it. More than once, she'd wondered if she would ever see him again.

When he neared, he didn't reach for her, didn't change expressions. He simply handed her a single page of white paper with a few typed words, a scrawled signature and a notary's stamp.

"What's this?" she asked, her gaze on him, not the paper.

"Read it."

Her fingers trembled as she took the page and began to read.

"Should Karen Hanson agree to marry me, I hereby relinquish any claim whatsoever against whatever property she might own at the time of our marriage. Such property shall be hers to do with as she chooses."

Stunned, she searched his face. "This is real?"

"They tell me it's legal," he said. "This time I had Miss Ames at the bank look me in the eye when I signed so there would be no mistaking that it was me. Nate Grogan was there, too. They still have a lot to make amends for after that last fiasco."

For a moment she was distracted. "Did they ever figure out who forged those papers?"

"No, and I told 'em to drop it. I'm convinced it was Jesse Oldham or someone he hired, but we might never know for sure no matter how much investigating is done."

She glanced again at the paper she held. "When did you do this?"

"Look at the date."

To her shock, it was dated back in the spring, long before the fire. Her hand went to her mouth. "Oh, Grady," she whispered, thinking of all the months he'd waited to show her this proof that she mattered more to him than the land. In all that time, he could so easily have changed his mind.

But he hadn't, she thought, lifting her gaze to his.

"It says something in here about marriage. Are you proposing?"

A smile tugged at his lips. "I suppose I did go about this a little backward, but I wanted you to be sure of one thing before we got into the other."

"Sure of what?" she asked, though it was clear as the blue Wyoming sky.

"That this is about the love I feel for you, about me wanting to spend the rest of my life with you." He reached into his pocket and withdrew a jeweler's box, then held it out to her. When she made no move to take it, he flipped it open to reveal a diamond solitaire, elegant in its simplicity, stunning in its confirmation that the proposal was for real. That diamond, its facets sparkling radiantly, all but shouted forever.

"Now, there's one more thing I want you to see before you decide yes or no," he said.

He reached into his back pocket this time and handed her a thick packet. When she opened it, she found airline tickets inside, two of them, to London. The date for travel was open, but the date of purchase, once again, was last spring. Her gaze flew to his.

"I thought it might be a good place to start our married life—someplace neutral, someplace romantic, someplace where I can show you that you're the only thing that matters to me," he explained.

"London," she breathed softly, tears stinging her eyes. "Oh, Grady, how did you know?"

He chuckled at the question. "That you wanted to go to London? The stack of travel brochures on the kitchen table way back when was my first clue, that and the fact that you've mentioned that dream a time or two. It wasn't hard."

"Not about London," she said, as she moved into his embrace and lifted her mouth to his. "How did you know the way to my heart?"

"Even easier," he said. "I looked into my own."

His mouth settled over hers then, coaxing, persuading, until she pulled away. Her heart thrumming, she glanced toward the ring he was still holding.

"I'm ready," she whispered. She had been for weeks, but she'd been too scared, too afraid that it might be too late.

His tanned fingers shook as he slid the ring onto her hand, then raised it to his lips. He gazed into her eyes, and only then did she see the hint of vulnerability fade, the quick rise of joy.

"For a while there, darlin', I was beginning to wonder if you ever would be."

"I'm sorry I took so long."

"You were worth the wait," he said, and then his mouth claimed hers once more.

Enemy, friend, lover...and now, one day soon, Grady would be her husband. Karen felt the familiar heat begin to build between them, felt the sharp tug of passion, and knew that this was right, that it was meant to be.

Epilogue

Karen gazed into the face of her son and felt an indescribable sense of joy steal over her. With his black hair and dark eyes, Thomas Grady Blackhawk was the most beautiful baby she'd ever seen.

His great-grandfather agreed with her. He'd been hovering over the two of them for days now, eager to take over feedings, even diaper changes. Watching the two of them together had been a revelation. Until then she had been just a tiny bit intimidated by Grady's grandfather. Now she knew that beneath that quiet, solemn, wise demeanor he was a real softie.

She also knew what she had to do. In fact, she had already talked to a lawyer and today, now that the christening was over and the guests had left, she would tell Grady and Thomas what she had decided.

There was a soft knock on the door of the nursery and both men came in. The baby whimpered as if he knew that his great-grandfather was in the vicinity. Only when she had handed him over to the old man did baby Thomas quiet down. She rose and gave them her place in the rocker, then walked over to the dresser to pick up the papers she had left there.

"What are those?" Grady asked.

She grinned as she handed them to him. "Why not read them and see for yourself?"

Regarding her with a puzzled expression, he took them and began to scan the contents. He'd barely read a page, when his gaze shot to hers. "You want to do this?"

"It's done."

"What is it?" Thomas asked.

"She's donated the ranch to the Bureau of Indian Affairs," Grady said. "It's to be a working ranch for Native American boys who need a second chance."

"The Blackhawk Ranch," she said quietly.

"But Caleb's family," Grady protested. "They'll hate this."

"I talked with them. I explained what I wanted to do and why. It was one of the most difficult conversations I've ever had in my life, but I told them I was prepared to go ahead with it whether they approved or not."

She reached for Grady's hand and pressed a kiss to his knuckles. "Do you know what his father said?"

Grady shook his head.

"He said it was the right thing to do, that if he hadn't been so blinded by his own anger and hurt all these years, he might have thought of it himself, that maybe if he had, Caleb would have been free to pursue a different life, that maybe he'd still be alive."

"And his mother?" Grady asked. "What did she say?"

"Not much that first time, but she called me the next day and told me it was okay. She said that loving your father might have been wrong, but that he had been a good man and this would be a fitting tribute to him. She also wanted me to ask if you could ever forgive her for blaming you for what happened the night your father died. She said it was a burden you never should have carried." Her eyes filled with tears. "After all this time, I think she and I have finally made peace."

"It's a fine thing you've done," Thomas said quietly. "But I think there's one change needed."

"What's that?" Grady asked.

"I think it should be the Blackhawk-Hanson Ranch. That would make it the real tribute it ought to be."

Karen had considered that, then dismissed it, fearing that it would negate the meaning of the gesture to Grady's ancestors. "Are you sure?" she asked, kneeling beside him.

Thomas Blackhawk rested his hand on her head in a gesture that was part blessing, part affection. "I'm very sure, child. No tribute to the past is complete if it ignores part of the history."

"Then the Blackhawk-Hanson Ranch it is," Grady said. "Maybe one day our son will grow up to run the place."

All three of them looked at the boy sleeping so peacefully in his great-grandfather's arms. He had quite a legacy to live up to, Karen thought, gazing from his father to his great-grandfather.

Then she grinned. The men in her life were really

something. And with Kenny Oldham spending so much of his time with them these days in an attempt to make up for his part in the fire, she was surrounded by males. She needed a daughter to even things up a bit. She met Grady's gaze.

"I think your grandfather has things under control in here," she began.

Grady grinned. "Absolutely. What did you have in mind?"

"Don't tell him in front of me," Thomas said. "I'm an old man. I don't need to know the details."

She winked at him. "Don't worry. I'll whisper my plans after I get him all alone."

A smile spread across the old man's face. "If he doesn't know without you spelling it out, he's no grandson of mine."

"I agree," Grady said, leading her from the room. "Talk is highly overrated."

"Then I'll show you," she said, closing their bedroom door securely behind her.

She was pretty sure he'd gotten the message even before her blouse hit the floor.

* * * * *

*Find out all about
the mysterious man who's been
pursuing Gina in*

TO CATCH A THIEF,

*on sale in September 2001
from Silhouette Special Edition.*

*Turn the page for
a sneak preview of*

TO CATCH A THIEF,

the third book in

THE CALAMITY JANES

series by Sherryl Woods.

Chapter One

"Gina Petrillo has gone *where?*" Rafe O'Donnell's head snapped up at his secretary's casual announcement.

"Wyoming. She called an hour ago and rescheduled the deposition," Lydia Allen repeated, looking entirely too cheerful.

If Rafe didn't know better, he'd think she was glad that this Gina person had escaped his clutches. He scowled at the woman who had been assigned to him when he first joined Whitfield, Mason and Lockhart seven years earlier. At the time, she'd been with the firm for twenty years and claimed she was always assigned to new recruits to make sure they were broken in properly. She was still with him, because she swore that to this day, he was too impossible to foist off on a less seasoned secretary.

"Did I say it was okay to reschedule?" he inquired irritably.

"You've been in court all day," she pointed out, clearly unintimidated by his sharp tone. "We reschedule these things all the time."

"Not so some crook can go gallivanting of to Wyoming," he snapped.

"You don't know that Gina Petrillo is a crook," Lydia chided. "Innocent until proved guilty, remember?"

Rafe held on to his temper by a thread. "I do not need to be lectured on the principles of law by a grandmother," he said, deliberately minimizing whatever legal expertise she might legitimately consider her due.

Typically, she ignored the insult. "Maybe not, but you could use a few hard truths. I've eaten at that restaurant. So have most of the partners in this firm. If you weren't such a workaholic, you'd probably be a regular there, too. The food is fabulous. Gina Petrillo is a lovely, beautiful young woman. She is not a thief."

So, he thought, that explained the attitude. Lydia was personally acquainted with the elusive woman and disapproved of Rafe's determination to link Gina Petrillo to her partner's crimes. As softhearted as his secretary was, she'd probably called Gina and warned her to get out of town.

"You say she's not a thief," he began with deceptive mildness in his best go-for-the-jugular mode. "Mind telling me how you reached that conclusion? Do you have a degree in psychology, perhaps? Access to the restaurant's books? Do you happen to have any evidence whatsoever that would actually exonerate her?''

''No, I do not have any evidence,'' she informed him with a huff. ''Neither do you. But, unlike some people, I am a very good judge of character, Rafe O'Donnell.''

Rafe was forced to concede that she was...usually.

''Now that Roberto,'' she continued, ''I can believe he's stolen from people. He has shifty eyes.''

''Thank you, Miss Marple,'' Rafe said snidely. ''Roberto Rinaldi was not the only one with access to the money.''

A good chunk of that money happened to belong to Rafe's socialite mother. She had been taken in by the man's charm. Rafe hadn't explored the exact nature of the relationship, but knowing his mother's track record, it hadn't been platonic. He was no more oblivious to his mother's faults than his father had been before the divorce, but he did his best to keep her from getting robbed blind.

''But Roberto is the one who's missing,'' Lydia pointed out. ''He's the one you should be concentrating on.''

''I would if I could find him,'' Rafe said, not bothering to hide his exasperation. ''Which is one reason I want to talk to Gina Petrillo. She just may know where he is. Now, thanks to you, I don't even know where *she* is.''

''Of course you do—I told you. She's gone to Wyoming.''

''It's a big state. Care to narrow it down?''

She frowned at him. ''There is no need to be sarcastic.''

Rafe sighed. ''Do you know where she is or not?''

"Of course I do."

"Then book me on the next flight."

"I doubt that Winding River has an airport. I'll check," she said, her expression unexpectedly brightening.

"Whatever," Rafe replied, not one bit happy about the images of western wilderness that came to mind. "Just cancel everything on my calendar and get me out there by tomorrow night."

"Will do, boss. I'll go ahead and cancel everything through next week. You could use the time off."

Lydia's sudden eagerness, the spring in her step as she started to leave his office, had him frowning. "I don't need time off," he protested. "I'll take care of this over the weekend and be back here on Monday."

"Why don't you just play it by ear?"

His gaze narrowed. "What are you up to?"

"Just doing my job," she said with an innocent expression.

Rafe seriously doubted her innocence, but for the life of him he couldn't figure out why Lydia was so blasted anxious for him to jet off to Wyoming. She was not the kind of secretary who used the boss's absence to sneak out and shop or even to take long lunch hours. No, she was the kind who meddled, the kind who took great pride in making his private life a living hell with her well-meant pestering.

And she liked this Gina Petrillo, he thought, suddenly making the connection.

"Lydia!" he bellowed.

"You don't have to shout," she scolded. "I'm just outside the door."

"When you book my room in Winding River, make sure I'm all alone in it."

She feigned shock. "Why, of course, I will."

"Don't look at me like that. It wouldn't be the first time some hotel mix-up had me sharing a room with a woman you thought I ought to get to know better."

"I never—"

"Save it, Just make sure of it, Lydia, or you'll spend the rest of your career at Whitfield, Mason and Lockhart doing the filing."

She shot him an unrepentant grin. "I doubt that, sir. I know where all the bodies are buried."

Rafe sighed heavily. She did, too.

Beloved author
Sherryl Woods
is back with a brand-new miniseries

THE CALAMITY JANES

Five women. Five Dreams.
A lifetime of friendship....

On Sale May 2001—DO YOU TAKE THIS REBEL?
Silhouette Special Edition

On Sale August 2001—COURTING THE ENEMY
Silhouette Special Edition

On Sale September 2001—TO CATCH A THIEF
Silhouette Special Edition

On Sale October 2001—THE CALAMITY JANES
Silhouette Single Title

On Sale November 2001—WRANGLING THE REDHEAD
Silhouette Special Edition

**"Sherryl Woods is an author who writes with
a very special warmth, wit, charm and intelligence."
—*New York Times* bestselling author
Heather Graham Pozzessere**

Available at your favorite retail outlet.

Where love comes alive™

Visit Silhouette at www.eHarlequin.com   SSETCJR

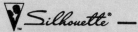

Don't miss this exciting new Silhouette Special Edition series from Laurie Paige!

Twenty years ago, tragedy struck the Windoms. Now the truth will be revealed with the power—and passion—of true love! Meet Kate, Shannon and Megan, three cousins who vow to restore the family name.

THE
WINDRAVEN
LEGACY

On sale May 2001
A stranger came, looking for a place to stay—
but what was he really looking for…? Find out why
Kate has **SOMETHING TO TALK ABOUT.**

On sale July 2001
An accident robbed Shannon of her sight, but a
neighbor refused to let her stay blind about her
feelings…in **WHEN I SEE YOUR FACE.**

On sale September 2001
Megan's memories of childhood had been lost.
Now she has a chance to discover the truth about
love…**WHEN I DREAM OF YOU.**

Available at your favorite retail outlet.

Silhouette®
Where love comes alive™

Visit Silhouette at www.eHarlequin.com

SSEWIND

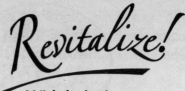

SILHOUETTE®
MAKES YOU
A STAR!

Feel like a star with Silhouette.

We will fly you and a guest to New York City for an exciting weekend stay at a glamorous 5-star hotel. Experience a refreshing day at one of New York's trendiest spas and have your photo taken by a professional. Plus, receive $1,000 U.S. spending money!

Flowers...long walks...dinner for two... how does Silhouette Books make romance come alive for you?

Send us a script, with 500 words or less, along with visuals (only drawings, magazine cutouts or photographs or combination thereof). Show us how Silhouette Makes Your Love Come Alive. Be creative and have fun. No purchase necessary. All entries must be clearly marked with your name, address and telephone number. All entries will become property of Silhouette and are not returnable. **Contest closes September 28, 2001.**

Please send your entry to: **Silhouette Makes You a Star!**

In U.S.A.
P.O. Box 9069
Buffalo, NY, 14269-9069

In Canada
P.O. Box 637
Fort Erie, ON, L2A 5X3

Look for contest details on the next page, by visiting www.eHarlequin.com or request a copy by sending a self-addressed envelope to the applicable address above. Contest open to Canadian and U.S. residents who are 18 or over. Void where prohibited.

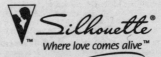

Silhouette®
Where love comes alive™

Our lucky winner's photo will appear in a Silhouette ad. Join the fun!

SRMYAS1

HARLEQUIN "SILHOUETTE MAKES YOU A STAR!" CONTEST 1308
OFFICIAL RULES
NO PURCHASE NECESSARY TO ENTER

1. To enter, follow directions published in the offer to which you are responding. Contest begins June 1, 2001, and ends on September 28, 2001. Entries must be postmarked by September 28, 2001, and received by October 5, 2001. Enter by hand-printing (or typing) on an 8 ½" x 11" piece of paper your name, address (including zip code), contest number/name and attaching a script containing <u>500 words or less, along with drawings, photographs or magazine cutouts, or combinations thereof</u> (i.e., collage) <u>on no larger than 9" x 12"</u> piece of paper, describing how the <u>Silhouette books make romance come alive for you.</u> Mail via first-class mail to: Harlequin "Silhouette Makes You a Star!" Contest 1308, (in the U.S.) P.O. Box 9069, Buffalo, NY 14269-9069, (in Canada) P.O. Box 637, Fort Erie, Ontario, Canada L2A 5X3. Limit one entry per person, household or organization.

2. Contests will be judged by a panel of members of the Harlequin editorial, marketing and public relations staff. Fifty percent of criteria will be judged against script and fifty percent will be judged against drawing, photographs and/or magazine cutouts. Judging criteria will be based on the following:

   - Sincerity—25%
   - Originality and Creativity—50%
   - Emotionally Compelling—25%

   In the event of a tie, duplicate prizes will be awarded. Decisions of the judges are final.

3. All entries become the property of Torstar Corp. and may be used for future promotional purposes. Entries will not be returned. No responsibility is assumed for lost, late, illegible, incomplete, inaccurate, nondelivered or misdirected mail.

4. Contest open only to residents of the U.S. <u>(except Puerto Rico)</u> and Canada who are 18 years of age or older, and is void wherever prohibited by law; all applicable laws and regulations apply. Any litigation within the Province of Quebec respecting the conduct or organization of a publicity contest may be submitted to the Régie des alcools, des courses et des jeux for a ruling. Any litigation respecting the awarding of a prize may be submitted to the Régie des alcools, des courses et des jeux only for the purpose of helping the parties reach a settlement. Employees and immediate family members of Torstar Corp. and D. L. Blair, Inc., their affiliates, subsidiaries and all other agencies, entities and persons connected with the use, marketing or conduct of this contest are not eligible to enter. Taxes on prizes are the sole responsibility of the winner. Acceptance of any prize offered constitutes permission to use winner's name, photograph or other likeness for the purposes of advertising, trade and promotion on behalf of Torstar Corp., its affiliates and subsidiaries without further compensation to the winner, unless prohibited by law.

5. Winner will be determined no later than November 30, 2001, and will be notified by mail. Winner will be required to sign and return an Affidavit of Eligibility/Release of Liability/Publicity Release form within 15 days after winner notification. Noncompliance within that time period may result in disqualification and an alternative winner may be selected. All travelers must execute a Release of Liability prior to ticketing and must possess required travel documents (e.g., passport, photo ID) where applicable. Trip must be booked by December 31, 2001, and completed within one year of notification. No substitution of prize permitted by winner. Torstar Corp. and D. L. Blair, Inc., their parents, affiliates and subsidiaries are not responsible for errors in printing of contest, entries and/or game pieces. In the event of printing or other errors that may result in unintended prize values or duplication of prizes, all affected game pieces or entries shall be null and void. **Purchase or acceptance of a product offer does not improve your chances of winning.**

6. Prizes: (1) Grand Prize—A 2-night/3-day trip for two (2) to New York City, including round-trip coach air transportation nearest winner's home and hotel accommodations (double occupancy) at The Plaza Hotel, a glamorous afternoon makeover at <u>a trendy New York spa</u>, $1,000 in U.S. spending money and an opportunity to <u>have a professional photo taken and appear in a Silhouette advertisement</u> (approximate retail value: $7,000). (10) Ten Runner-Up Prizes of gift packages (retail value $50 ea.). Prizes consist of only those items listed as part of the prize. Limit one prize per person. Prize is valued in U.S. currency.

7. For the name of the winner (available after December 31, 2001) send a self-addressed, stamped envelope to: Harlequin "Silhouette Makes You a Star!" Contest 1197 Winners, P.O. Box 4200 Blair, NE 68009-4200 or you may access the www.eHarlequin.com Web site through February 28, 2002.

Contest sponsored by Torstar Corp., P.O. Box 9042, Buffalo, NY 14269-9042.

SRMYAS2

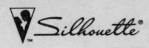

COMING NEXT MONTH